"I am uncertain a... ...ssist me in determining ... ...s?"

"No, of course I do, but—okay." Kim took a deep breath. "Ravens or some other black bird, huh?"

"Correct."

Kim cocked his head and thought. "Edgar Allan Poe. Nevermore. *The Twa Corbies. Sing a Song of Sixpence.* The Ugly Duckling. No, wait, he turned into a swan. Umm. . . ."

But Seven had gone cold inside. Around her, a chorus of shrieking birds had suddenly appeared. They were flying about, their wings flapping, hugely excited.

Yes. *Sing a song of sixpence, a pocket full of rye; four and twenty blackbirds—*

Pain ripped through her, exquisite in its agony. That awful smell of carrion filled her nostrils and twisted her stomach into knots. Her knees buckled and with a low groan she collapsed. Harry seized her elbows and tried to lift her. She heard his voice, but faintly, as if he were far away: "Seven? Seven, are you all right?"

Why was he calling her Seven? She was the First of Six in her household—that was, until the Great Destroyers came. And his face—hideous! Deformed! Frantically, Amari seized his face and cried out, "What have the Destroyers done to you? Oh, my love, my love. . . ." She kissed him, and when she pulled back, Sulmi's face was again the handsome, feathered visage she so adored. His expression was confused, and the words he spoke were curious:

"Doctor, I'm bringing Seven in right now. It's happening again."

STAR TREK VOYAGER®

SEVEN OF NINE

Christie Golden

POCKET BOOKS

New York London Toronto Sydney Tokyo Singapore

An *Original* Publication of POCKET BOOKS

POCKET BOOKS, a division of Simon & Schuster Inc.
1230 Avenue of the Americas, New York, NY 10020

This book is published by Pocket Books, a division of Simon & Schuster Inc., under exclusive license from Paramount Pictures.

ISBN: 0-671-02491-4

First Pocket Books printing September 1998

10 9 8 7 6 5 4 3 2 1

Printed in the U.S.A.

This book is dedicated,
appropriately enough,
to Raven Moore

SEVEN OF NINE

PROLOGUE

TAMAAK VRIIS STARED AT THE SCREEN AND DRUMMED HIS three fingers on the console.

Nothing. Only the blackness of space, punctuated by the twinkling of a few stars, met his gaze.

He felt a blackness of his own rising within him; despair, mixed with the dark indigo of fear. His colleague, Imraak, the elected One of the province of Leila'ah, glanced at him sharply. The numbing darkness of despair mutated into the heat of embarrassment. Normally, Tamaak, the elected One of the vast continent of Ioh and the selected leader of the entire Circle of Seven, was adept at cloaking his thoughts. He, more than most, knew how a stray image could disturb the harmony the Skedans valued above all qualities.

He sent a cooling, feather-brush apology, and Imraak nodded his acceptance. On Tamaak's other side, staring intently into her own screen, Shemaak shook her graceful head. Her huge ears flickered, revealing her own distress, though her thoughts remained calm.

They ought to be here by now, Shemaak sent. The enclosed room felt colder as the Seven heard and reacted to her comment. *Our scouts died to relay the information of the attack, and the Emperor promised to send reinforcements for our defense fifty sun circles ago.*

Again, silence. Shemaak had merely given utterance to what they all feared. There was nothing more to say. Slowly, heads turned and large brown eyes regarded their leader. Tamaak felt the press of their worry like a too-heavy blanket on a hot summer day.

He collected his thoughts and sent them. *We have done what we can. The attack should not come for another six sun circles. In that time, the Emperor's fleet will certainly have arrived. In the meantime, we—*

Imraak's uncensored anger was like a physical blow and they all gasped softly with the pain of his sending. *He will not send help! We all know this. If it was to come, it would have come by now. The attack will—*

His white-hot anger was disrupted by the insistent, mechanical beeping of the main viewing screen. They all turned to stare.

The attack had come. Early.

Anguish exploding from seven master telepaths made the room feel so close each breath was a struggle. Skedan technology was advanced. There was no mistaking the images that now swarmed onto the screen. Large, square cubes, bristling with sharp gray edges. Crawling with beings that were an offense to She-Who-Creates—monstrous hybrids of the biological, the natural, and the technological, the artificial. Beings without conscience, without souls, who descended like the wrath of He-Who-Destroys to obliterate entire species.

The despair and rage and pain that nearly ripped Tamaak apart was not for himself. It was for his people—people who, betrayed by the Empire with which they had allied, had no natural defense systems of their own. People who had elected him as leader of the Circle of Seven, who had counted on him for protection. He realized what must have happened. This unnatural enemy had gotten to the scout ships, had learned what the unfortunate scouts had learned, and had doubled their speed to reach Skeda early in order to catch the peaceful planet unprepared.

People didn't even have the chance to flee into the shelters that had been hastily dug. They were on their way to the gardens and fields, no doubt looking up and sending off wave after wave of shocked terror before the foe descended.

Tamaak thought of Rhiv, his mate, and their two little ones. They would be among those walking towards the green fields, who had time to look their deaths in the face. Thoughts alone could not let him grieve properly, and a scream tore from his throat.

The voice, a dark harmony of millions of voices, crackled through the silent room.

"We are the Borg. Prepare to be assimilated. Your biological and technological distinctiveness will be added to our own. Resistance is futile."

CHAPTER 1

"THAT'S THE BIGGEST PIECE OF CLAIMED SPACE I'VE EVER
seen!" blurted Lieutenant Tom Paris as he and the
rest of the senior staff stood gathered in Astrometrics.
Before them on the huge screen was a grid displaying
a particular area of space. Even though the grid had
been scaled down dramatically, the mapped area
filled the screen.

"That's why it's called an empire," said Lieutenant
B'Elanna Torres, softening the gibe with a smile.

"Well, yeah, but—wow! I mean, look at it!"

"Crossing through it, even at its narrowest point,
will take several weeks. And circumnavigating it
would take almost a year." Captain Kathryn Janeway

crossed her arms and glared at the vast expanse of the Lhiaarian Empire, an imperfect circle of pale blue on the map.

Paris had used colorful terms, but he was essentially correct. It *was* the single biggest area of claimed space that any of them had ever seen. It made the Romulan and Klingon empires look like anthills. Janeway suspected that the Borg's area of dominance would give the Lhiaarrian Empire a run for its money, but Seven of Nine had not been forthcoming with any details. Besides, the Borg considered the entire universe their empire—they just hadn't charted all of it yet.

"Mr. Neelix, what do you have on the Lhiaari for me?"

The Talaxian perked up at the mention of his name and strode forward. He examined his padd with a flourish. "Well, as we can see, it's quite the, ah, piece of space, isn't it? The term Lhiaarian Empire is actually something of a misnomer. The Lhiaari only live on a single planet, which is their homeworld and the capital of the empire, located about . . ."

He delicately tapped the console and the mapped area shifted, zooming in on a single orb. It looked so much like Earth it made Janeway's heart skip a beat. "Here. They are an intelligent race, not overly given to warfare, and quite advanced. However, they do seem inordinately fond of red tape.

"The entire perimeter of their space is loaded with checkpoints, and there are more sprinkled about here, here, and here. Apparently, it can sometimes take weeks for ships to negotiate passage if a vessel hasn't been given express clearance by Emperor Beytek himself."

"That is unacceptable." Seven of Nine stood erect at the console. Her face, pale, blue-eyed, and graced with a few remnants of Borg technology, was almost as unreadable as that of Commander Tuvok, the Vulcan security officer who stood silently beside her. The blue light from the screen played across her features, glinting on the metal of her implants.

"We do not have the resources to sit idly in space-dock awaiting clearance."

"Hate to say it, but I'm with Seven on this one," said Torres. "Isn't there something we can do?"

"There are times on this journey when I would rather have a good old-fashioned firefight than keep kowtowing to the diplomats," said Janeway, a smile crinkling the corners of her eyes. "And right now is one of them. This sounds like the Bowmar all over again. But I don't see any other alternative. I'm not going to add an entire year to our journey just because we don't want to be annoyed by red tape. Neelix, how are we doing on foodstuffs?"

The Talaxian's dappled brow furrowed. "We're doing all right on seasonings, but staples are dipping below my comfort level. We haven't passed through any space where we could stop to replenish our supplies. There is of course always the replicator and rations if we get into a tight spot."

"Rations. Mmmmm," said Harry Kim, rolling his eyes.

"If we are going to be stalled in space, twiddling our

thumbs at an emperor's whim for a week or two, I would respectfully request that the replicator be reserved for medicines and medical supplies," put in the Doctor.

"Now wait a minute," interrupted Torres, turning with a frown. "Engineering needs—"

"That's enough!" Janeway's voice held an edge. "We're not even in Imperial space yet and already we're arguing about who gets the replicators! Tom, how far are we from the first checkpoint?"

"We should be there in a few hours if we maintain present speed, Captain." Janeway smothered a smile. Paris looked like a choirboy, eyes wide and guileless, careful to not attract attention after Janeway had just reprimanded the others.

"Do it. We'll see if we can't hurry up passage to the next point after this one. Perhaps we can manage an audience with the Emperor and get a hold of one of those coveted free passes. I think a ship from another quadrant might be something Emperor Beytek would be interested in seeing. Seven, do the Borg know anything about this species? Anything that might give us an edge in negotiating with them?"

Janeway had asked the question deliberately. Though Seven was human now—well, mostly human; eighteen per cent of her body was still cyborg technology—she had been raised by the Borg and had no doubt personally committed more than her share of atrocities in the name of assimilation. It was simply a part of who she was, and Janeway was determined that, eventually, her crew would get used to that fact. Though the information Seven harbored was gleaned in a monstrous fashion, it was still information. Much of what Seven knew about various species had proved helpful in the past. Once, in the case of the Katati, it had even given them the means to evade destruction and to make some kind of reparation to a race the Borg had decimated. And the knowledge of Species 149 had brought Neelix back from the dead. Janeway liked those kinds of ironies.

Seven arched a pale eyebrow. "The Lhiaari were not assimilated by the Borg in the time that I was with them. The name is known to me, however, because we assimilated the inhabitants of some of their conquered worlds who dislike and distrust the Emperor."

"Not an unusual attitude, for the inhabitants of a conquered world," Chakotay said quietly. Janeway smiled sympathetically at her first officer, then looked at the screen. She moved forward, touched the console, and restored the full image of the circle of the Lhiaarian Empire.

They had to find a way through. Janeway knew that she would lay down her life for her crew. Such a sentiment was nothing out of the ordinary for a good starship captain. But she was also prepared to swallow her pride if it meant getting them a year closer to home. She'd bow and scrape and smile and do whatever was necessary to win passage through this mammoth area of claimed space.

That was a lot harder than taking a phaser blast.

"Stations, everyone. According to Mr. Paris, we should be arriving at the first checkpoint inside Lhiaarian space at 1400 hours. Let's put our best foot forward."

Out of the corner of her eye, Janeway saw Seven of Nine looking down at her feet with a puzzled frown.

Seven of Nine, personal log: I do not understand the human fondness for what they refer to as "slang." It is inefficient and leads to confusion and misunderstandings. However, I am attempting to integrate such terms into my vocabulary matrix and cross-reference them in order to facilitate conversing with this crew. Lieutenant Paris seems to be an inexhaustible reservoir of various bizarre terms.

The Lhiaari have already proven Mr. Neelix's observations of them to be accurate. Rather than send a delegation aboard Voyager, *they have required that we beam down to the planet's surface and submit our request through certain established channels. Mr. Paris says this makes us "sheep." I am uncertain as to how obeying protocol transforms humanoids into ovines, but I shall observe and hope that he is incorrect. I do not think I would like to be an ovine.*

"My God," breathed Janeway. "This is worse than I thought."

"Ellis Island must have looked like this back in the nineteenth century," said Paris, glancing around. "Bring me your tired, your poor, your huddled masses. I'd say this qualifies as a huddled mass."

"More like a huddled mess," said Janeway. Frowning, she tapped her commbadge. "Janeway to *Voyager.*"

"Chakotay here. What's the situation?"

"Looks like we're going to be here a while." It was an understatement. They had beamed into the midst of a swirling sea of people. Some were humanoid, some most definitely weren't. Some of them practiced . . . different hygiene from those aboard *Voyager*. All of them were loud and apparently annoyed. Janeway almost had to shout to be heard above the din. Her translator struggled to interpret the various yelps, groans, squeaks, whistles, and purrs and finally, exasperated, Janeway yelled, "I'll update you as necessary, Chakotay. I'm turning off my commbadge and so is the rest of the away team." And she did.

Her team of Paris, Seven, Kim, and Tuvok imitated her, grimacing at the noise and smells into which they had found themselves abruptly plunged. A faint ripple of displeasure marred even the normally tranquil surface of Tuvok's face.

Seven of Nine glanced about with curiosity. The place, a poorly lit and poorly ventilated single chamber, was crammed with bodies. There were clearly supposed to be lines, but such niceties had been ignored, probably for some time. A few scanning booths, designed to detect weapons or unauthorized communications devices, were set up at various locations. Few people seemed to be passing through without a lot of very loud arguments.

Seven recognized many of the alien life forms present at this waystation. There was a member of Species 2822, approaching the bored, irritated, and apparently hungry people in line with some sort of food. They were a species which thrived on opportunity, surviving apparently devastating natural disasters with ingenuity and skill. Their distinctiveness was added to the Borg several decades ago.

Over there was a cluster of Species 1811. Not added; dismissed as unworthy. They would have weakened the whole. They did not adapt well to the rigors required of the drones and died quickly.

"This line does not appear to be moving with any rapidity," observed Tuvok.

"This line does not appear to be moving at all," said Paris, "nor does it appear to even be a *line*. Captain, this is ridiculous. It could be hours before we even get to talk to anyone."

"At the rate in which the line is progressing forward," said Tuvok coolly, "it would be nine point seven hours."

Janeway sighed deeply and rubbed her temples. "Any suggestions? I'd rather wait nine point seven hours than spend a year going around the Empire's space."

Idle chitchat and complaints. Something that Seven had observed comprised a great deal of human conversation. She returned her attention to the crowd. Analyzing the variety of life before her was more interesting than listening to her crewmates squabble.

She narrowed her eyes. A small group of Species 4774 had noticed them and was now pushing through the crowd in their direction.

"Captain," said Seven. "We are being approached by—"

"I see them, Seven," said Janeway. The aliens took a few more moments—the press of the crowd was tight—but it was clear that the five members of the *Voyager* crew were the object of their interest. At last, one who appeared to be their leader stood before them.

Species 4774. Known as the Skedans. A race of telepaths with a protective ridge of bone on the skull that protrudes down the back. Non-aggressive. Resistance was minimal. The young are inefficiently nurtured in pouches. Physically, they did not make good drones, but their telepathic abilities were analyzed and added to the technological and biological distinctiveness of the Borg.

The alien looked at them expectantly, and uttered a series of whistles and clicks. Belatedly, Janeway seemed to remember that they had switched off their communicator/translators and quickly activated hers. She smiled at the alien, but the smile grew quizzical as she sniffed the air. Janeway shook her head and chuckled. "If I didn't know better, I'd say someone was brewing coffee." Seven marveled, not for the first time, at the human capacity for distraction.

"I'm sorry, our translators weren't active. Can you repeat what you just said, please?" asked Janeway, apparently shaking herself out of her reverie.

"Certainly. Please excuse the intrusion. You are Captain Janeway of the Alpha Quadrant vessel *Voyager?*"

Janeway nodded. "Yes. And you are . . . ?"

The alien bowed deeply. "I am Tamaak Vriis. I have a favor to ask, and a favor to offer."

"I'm listening."

"My people," and he gestured to the cluster of

thirty-odd large-eyed beings who stood respectfully behind him, "are without a home. We Skedans are good citizens of the Lhiaarian Empire, and we are attempting to reach the Emperor and ask for repatriation. You are also seeking passage through Imperial space, or you would not be here. If I can move you swiftly through all the checkpoints, will you give my people passage to Lhiaari aboard your vessel?"

"Tamaak, if you can speed up this process, I might let you *pilot* the vessel," said Janeway, hope lighting her face. "But I don't see how—"

Tamaak turned his head and half-closed his eyes. A few seconds later, one of the heavily armored, burly, four-armed aliens who served as guards in the place trundled up to them.

"Captain Janeway?"

"Yes?"

"Your admission requirements are being addressed. Please, follow me."

They all turned to stare at Tamaak, mouths open with shock, then hastened to follow the guard before he was swallowed up by the crowd.

Seven was unimpressed. Janeway and the others did not know of the Skedan's formidable telepathic powers. Clearly, he had "suggested" to the guard that the *Voyager* crew should be given priority. She followed, the last in line, pushing her way through the crowd. For a moment, she lost sight of the black-and-red uniform of her captain, and craned to see her.

A horrible scent assaulted her nostrils. It was the rank, stomach-churning stench of rotting flesh. Suddenly fear squeezed her heart, sent adrenaline spurting through her. Seven's mouth went dry.

No . . . not again . . . .

Straight ahead, perched atop a scanning booth and impaling her with its yellow-eyed gaze, was an enormous black bird.

CHAPTER

2

JANEWAY COULDN'T BELIEVE THEIR LUCK. SHE WASN'T sure exactly what kind of connections Tamaak Vriis had, but whatever they were they were certainly welcome. They made quite a sizable group, the refugees and the delegation from the Federation starship, as they followed behind the Imperial guard. Out of the corner of her eye, Janeway allowed herself the chance for a better look at her benefactor and his people.

They were a little smaller than humans, and though they were certainly bipedal, they weren't exactly humanoid. What once must have been an elongated, cervine muzzle eons ago had compressed into a

16

smaller version on a flatter, more humanoid face. The eyes were enormous, soft and limpid. The skull was large and protected by a covering of bone which extended down the beings' backs.

They had arms with three fingers that appeared dexterous enough, and a delicate torso flared into large hindquarters with powerful legs. Soft, pale brown fur covered those body parts not protected by bone. All of the Skedans carried heavy packs. Clearly the skeletal and muscular structure, reinforced by the bone ridge down their back, made them quite strong despite an almost fragile appearance.

A soft chirp caused Janeway to glance over at another of the Skedans. It was a female, and one of her young poked its head up out of a pouch in her belly. It was adorable, its big eyes and ears reminding Janeway of a fawn. Its mother picked it up and cradled it, murmuring, her eyes catching Janeway's and half-closing in what Janeway somehow knew to be the equivalent of a friendly smile.

Janeway smiled back, though her heart suddenly ached with sympathy. The children always suffered the most in tragic situations like this one, but clearly the Skedans were a loving, supportive family unit. She liked them immediately, feeling a deep and profound sense of kinship with them even though they were so unlike humans in their appearances.

"Captain." Tuvok's cool voice broke her train of thought. "We have lost Seven."

"What?" Janeway stopped so abruptly that Paris

almost walked into her. She craned her neck to see and worry gnawed at her. Tuvok, as usual, was right. Seven was nowhere to be found.

"Captain? Our guide is rapidly outpacing us," Tamaak said.

"Sorry, Tamaak, we've lost a member of our crew in the crowd. Excuse me." She hurried forward to catch one of the guard's four arms. "We'll have to wait a moment. One of our crewmembers is missing."

"Wait, I see her," said Kim. "I'll go get her."

Janeway watched him go, the pleasant company of her new friends forgotten in a wash of concern over Seven of Nine. Then logic reasserted itself. Of any member of her crew, Seven could probably take care of herself with the most efficiency. She'd be all right. Probably she'd just spotted something of interest and taken off to examine it without thinking to request permission. It would be just like her.

The humans had a term for this phenomenon. They called it *déjà vu,* which meant "already seen" in one of their Earth languages. *French,* a calm part of her mind told her with irritating irrelevance, even as she sat huddled against the wall, long legs clasped to her chest.

It seems to know me. Those were the words she had entered in her log almost a year ago, when the visions of the black bird—the raven—began haunting her. The mystery of her visions and the concurrent regeneration of the nanoprobes lying dormant in her blood-stream had been solved then. Seven had been responding to a Borg resonance signal, a kind of homing beacon.

The signal had led her to the wreckage of the only home she had known until she had been assimilated—a small Federation vessel piloted by her parents. That vessel was called the *Raven*. The Borg signal had reawakened both her implants and her memories. The Doctor had adjusted her implants so that she would not be troubled by Borg resonance in the future.

Or so they had all thought.

She raised her head and stared again at the bird. It really did seem to know her. It had flown closer now, and stared, unblinking, into her blue eyes.

"You are nothing more than a product of my—my imagination," Seven told it sternly. She fought to keep her voice from quivering, her body from trembling. She failed. "You are not real. You do not exist!"

The blackbird opened its beak as if in silent laughter.

"Look, mama!" Seven cried, extending a pale blue digit in the direction of the bird. "It's a skorrak! They're not supposed to be here for seventeen more circles!"

"You've been studying hard, Keela!" Her mother, soft and warm and furry, stroked her daughter with a clawed hand. Seven snuggled into the embrace, loving to be touched and petted. "Your tutor must be

very proud. Now, are you going to make Warrior K'itka proud too? Bring him the first skorrak of the season?"

Nervousness caused Seven's two hearts to beat faster, but she set her pointed teeth and nodded.

"I will do my best," she assured her mother.

"That is all I would ever ask, my dear child."

The soft, yellow tufts of fur about Seven's eyes and jaw fluttered softly with the gesture. Normally, when she went hunting, she carried weapons, but it was the mark of a true warrior to bring down prey with only his hands and teeth and wits. Perhaps today would be the day of her first blooding. It was an exciting thought.

The skorrak remained unaware of their presence. It hopped about on its spindly legs, its scarlet and black plumage gleaming in the early morning light. Seven settled herself, and focused on the prey. Her long tail twitched, revealing her agitation. Then she leaped forward, propelled by the power of her enormous haunches, and landed on the bird. It squawked and managed to elude her clumsy, kitten's pounce. All Seven got for her trouble was a mouthful of feathers.

"Seven, are you okay?"

Seven blinked. Her head felt like it weighed a hundred kilos, far too heavy for her slender stalk of a neck. It was Harry Kim, of course. Trust him to be the one to come find her. He seemed to be both afraid and protective of her. There was a slang term—behaving like a mother hen with—

with a single skorrak chick.

"Ah!" She gasped and pressed her fingers to her temples.

"Seven, what is it?"

Fear rushed through Keela. Where was she? Where was her mother, the brightly hued skorrak? Something had happened. Something frightening. The ugly face peering down at her, which had hardly any proper muzzle at all and was stripped of its beautiful fur, was still somehow familiar. Comforting. She could trust the owner of the unsightly face.

Keela launched herself upward into the stranger/friend's arms, sobbing. Fresh horror ripped through her as she realized that somehow she had been transformed from her proper, graceful feline shape into this bizarre and alien one. The thing's paws went around her, warm and strong. It uttered words she knew and did not know:

"Kim to *Voyager*. Emergency medical beam-up *now*."

"I'm afraid I'm at a loss to explain this," said the Doctor. His brow furrowed. Clearly, it irritated him.

Kim fought back a wave of irritation of his own. It had moved him more than he cared to admit when Seven of Nine had reached for him, tears—tears!—wet on her face, her eyes wide. He had gathered her in his arms as they beamed back to *Voyager* and gently placed her on the diagnostic bed himself. She was still looking about with terror on her beautiful face, whimpering.

"Is it the same thing that happened to her before—with the *Raven?*" asked Harry, his eyes glued to the image of the proud and competent woman caught in the grip of something he couldn't understand.

"If it were," replied the Doctor crossly, "I'd know what it was, wouldn't I? There are some similar symptoms—the agitated hippocampus, for example. Fortunately, this time the patient is crouched in a fetal position on the diagnostic bed, not slamming security guards into bulkheads and breaking through closed shuttlebay doors."

Kim didn't say anything, but silently, he thought he'd prefer the latter. Seven's anger, her arrogance, her—her Borgness—he understood, to some extent. This, he didn't. And it scared the hell out of him.

Then, even as he watched, something passed over her face. Her body straightened out, relaxed. Her face settled into its usual expression, a combination of calmness and near-disdain.

"Doctor." Not a plaintive call from a frightened patient, just a blunt statement.

"Yes, Seven." The Doctor replied in kind.

"I am in sickbay?"

"Yes." The Doctor's gaze shot to Harry, then back to Seven.

"I am damaged?"

"Depends on how you look at it." He pressed a button and the diagnostic bed's curving metal arc receded. Seven set up, her back perfectly straight, as usual. "Do you remember anything about what happened?"

Something flickered over her face, like a cloud passing across the sun. Then she was again composed.

"I believe I was hallucinating."

"Was it the same experience as the last episode? When you were drawn by the Borg resonance signal to the *Raven?*"

"Yes . . . and no. Have the dormant nanoprobes been reactivated?"

The Doctor shook his head. "Thank heaven for small favors," he said. "Physically, you show no signs of damage, disease, or anything out of the ordinary, except for a higher-than-normal production of adrenaline and endorphins. And I believe that was triggered by this hallucination. Were you in danger? Were the Borg chasing you?"

"No. The Borg were not present at all. I was—my name was Keela. I was a felinoid being, hunting birds with my mother. It was very pleasant, until . . ."

She broke off. Harry saw her swallow, saw her hands clench almost imperceptibly. He ached to put a supportive arm around her shoulders, but didn't dare.

"Until Ensign Kim spoke to me."

"Why was that bad?" asked Kim, trying not to let the hurt show.

"Because it made me aware of my human form. Physically, I was Seven of Nine. But it was as if Keela was trapped inside this body. She—I—was terrified. We were both present simultaneously."

"Was there anything that triggered this?" pressed the Doctor. "A smell, a sound, an image—anything that might have made you conjure a felinoid creature? It's a rather unusual choice of hallucination."

"The bird," said Seven, softly.

"The bird you were hunting?"

"No, the bird . . . the black bird. It was there, in the

middle of the admissions room—perched on one of the scanning booths. Staring right at me. The same one from—from before."

Harry felt his skin erupt in gooseflesh. Seven's fear crept into her voice, into her body language, though she struggled not to let it show.

"The raven?" Even the Doctor was concerned. He eyed his medical tricorder. "Well, well. Your adrenaline level just went up again."

Big surprise, thought Kim.

"I know this is difficult for you, but we must discuss it. Did the raven appear as part of the hallucination?"

"No. It was there, in the admissions chambers, as real as Captain Janeway or the guards." Her lids lowered over her eyes. "At least, it appeared real."

"Let me make sure I understand this," said the Doctor, pacing unhappily. "The raven appeared to be real, and then you experienced the hallucination in which the raven did *not* appear?"

"That is correct."

"There are days when deleting my program seems like a good idea," growled the Doctor. "Oh, to be a pleasure hologram like Mr. Paris's pirates. Nonetheless, luckily for you, I'm programmed with a greater sense of responsibility." He sobered, then sighed. "Seven, I frankly see no reason why you should be having these hallucinations, and I find it quite vexing that you are. You appear fit to return to duty. And brooding in your alcove probably wouldn't do much good. But you must contact me if you have any more dreams about your lost kittenhood, or see any ominous black birds."

Seven tensed. Her breathing became quick, and her voice trembled.

"Then, Doctor, I must alert you now."

Kim gasped. The Doctor snapped to attention at once, his tricorder humming. "You're hallucinating? Seeing a raven?"

"Neither." Her voice broke. "I am seeing *two* ravens."

CHAPTER

3

THE MESSAGE INDICATOR LIGHT WAS FLASHING PALE green.

Delayed by time and distance, news of the quarry had eventually arrived, as Kraa T'Krr had known it would. His people had been employed in their present positions by many worlds, for many centuries, because however long the task might take, in the end they never failed.

Kraa's antennae waved in happy anticipation and he extended a thin, spine-covered leg to activate the message. Settling back on his rear appendages, a position he could comfortably hold for hours, he waited for the Observer's report. He closed his compound eyes to avoid distraction; his three simple eyes would best comprehend the flickering lights of the message.

"O most gracious commander, Killer of the Warms, Slayer of those who are not holy, Victor of the battle of . . ." Kraa listened patiently, staring at the dancing lights that comprised the easiest and most precise form of communication between Tuktaks. This particular Observer was stationed in the Sella sector, on one of the Imperial waystations. Their target must be getting desperate to actually venture onto Imperial territory. Finally the Observer finished the obligatory accolades that played such a vital part in Tuktak society and got to the heart of the matter.

"They have been spotted, on Waystation Number 38. We did nothing, as you requested, and they did not see us. They were thirty-two in number, sixteen males, ten females, and six of their disgusting young." The messenger's silver-blue antennae waved in uncontrollable distress and even Kraa had to suppress revulsion. All Warms were nauseating to him, but particularly the larval stages of this species.

"They obtained passage on a vessel from the Alpha Quadrant, known as *Voyager*. The predominant race are Warms called humans, and nearly all aboard the ship are Warms. There seems to be no indication that their captain, a female named Janeway, is aware of their true nature or status. They were last seen heading mark seven-four-two point eight."

Directly toward the Lhiarri homeworld, thought Kraa, growing uneasy.

"Their preferred gravity is nine point eight-one T/sm; their air is a mixture of nitrogen, oxygen, and carbon dioxide—perfectly breathable for us. This is all I know, Commander. This Observer has reported."

The colored lights blipped and faded. Kraa absently began to clean his left antenna with his first pair of legs, moistening it and scraping it with the occasional nibble from his mandibles. The sensation was pleasant. It soothed him and helped him concentrate.

The difference in gravity would not be a problem. Centuries ago, interacting with most developed Warms on their native planets would have killed the Tuktak. Under such gravity, most insects remained small. The Tuktak had developed under lower gravity. On planets where Warms were the dominant intelligent race, the weight of the Tuktak's own exoskeletons would have crushed them.

But that was before they developed technology and learned that they could alter the natural progression of sclerotization. By supplementing their diet with artificially designed proteins, the Tuktak could precisely control the density of their exoskeletons. Kraa had been cultivating a lighter exoskeleton since his last shedding. He and the Tuktak under his command were all able to exist under Warm gravity.

When you could compete with the Warms on their own terms, pursuit and killing became much simpler.

Kraa reached his decision. The vessel designated *Voyager* had the advantage of lead time, but they would have to stop at the Imperial checkpoints. Such points were well known to Kraa. Having to stop and undergo the tedious process of registration at each checkpoint would slow this interfering Alpha Quadrant vessel greatly.

Eventually, the Tuktak would catch up with them and complete the task they were set: to destroy, at all costs, the Skedans and anyone who knew about them.

He leaned forward, touched the console and sent a message to his crew.

"The Doctor tells me you've been having hallucinations," said Janeway without preamble.

Seven glanced up from the console, met her captain's eyes, and nodded acknowledgment. "That is correct."

"I don't suppose you'd like to talk about it?" Janeway stepped closer, reached a hand toward Seven's shoulder, then clearly thought better of the gesture.

"No. I do not. I have told the Doctor everything I recall." Her eyes flickered from her rapidly moving fingers to the black bird that sat on the console. It opened its beak and squawked. "Except . . ."

"Yes?"

When Seven turned to look at her visitor, she saw the second bird had taken up residence on Janeway's shoulder. The captain appeared to notice nothing amiss, just as the Doctor and Harry had been unable to see the birds in sickbay. The third bird hopped busily along the floor, picking at food that was as imaginary as it was.

"The number of birds I am seeing is increasing."

Janeway's brow furrowed in concern. "Do you see them now?"

"Yes. There are three of them. One on the floor, one on the console, and one on your right shoulder."

Seven felt a brief flicker of mirth as Janeway involuntarily started and glanced down at her shoulder. The bird that was perched there stared back at her.

"They are with me constantly. However, I find that I am able to continue working despite their presence. Much the way that I am able to perform to expectations despite Mr. Kim's occasional behavioral eccentricities."

"Mr. Kim's . . ." Janeway shook her head and let the subject drop. "Seven, I have to tell you, I'm quite concerned about this."

"There is nothing to be concerned about, Captain. I am displaying none of the physical symptoms that occurred previously. My nanoprobes are dormant, and I feel no desire to injure the crew or leave the vessel. The birds are nothing but an annoyance. They are in fact easier to ignore than humans," she added pointedly.

Janeway opened her mouth, then her eyes lit on the screen. She frowned. "Seven, what are you analyzing?"

"I am plotting our course to the Lhiarri homeworld and incorporating all waystation points, as I have been ordered, of cou—" Seven broke off abruptly, her gaze following Janeway's.

What was on the screen was not the area of space that lay before them. It was a small spot of space hundreds of light-years away. Seven knew that area, and fear spurted adrenaline into her human bloodstream.

"What is it?" Janeway moved closer and though Seven didn't want to admit it, her presence was suddenly a comfort.

Seven licked dry lips. "It is the homeworld and owned space of the Graa. Keela's race."

"I think you'd better report back to sickbay."

"Captain, I am weary of being analyzed by the Doctor," Seven retorted, and Janeway's lips curved in a smile.

"I can see that," said the captain. "But I don't want you here at the moment." She gestured at the grid on the screen. "You're in a position where an error could be disastrous. Surely you can understand that."

"I have failed you. I am . . ." Seven reached for the word Torres had taught her. "Sorry." Her voice, as always, was clipped and cool. Inside, though, she raged. The sensation was as alien as it was powerful.

"Seven, you're undergoing something terribly traumatic, made all the worse by the fact that no one knows what it is. I wouldn't call it failure. Why don't you take a break and return to your alcove for a few hours? I'll come talk to you later and see how you're feeling."

It was couched as a suggestion, but Seven had learned to know a command when she heard one. She nodded, and without further comment turned and left Astrometrics. The door hissed shut behind her. But the birds followed.

She had no intention of arguing with Janeway, and the incident in Astrometrics had unsettled her as well. Seven of Nine fully intended to return to her alcove and spend a few hours regenerating. But just as her fingers had betrayed her in Astrometrics, calling up one area of space while she intended to research another, now her feet seemed to have a will of their own. She strode down the corridors, the three black birds flying silently ahead of her leading the way.

She stopped in front of the entrance to Holodeck Two and requested a certain program.

"Simulation activated," came the brisk female voice of the computer, and the doors opened.

It was morning in Tuscany. The light flooded Leonardo da Vinci's studio, and dust motes swirled in the golden glow. The three black birds happily settled themselves, almost as much a part of the environment as the paintings, sculptures, and models they adorned.

Seven blinked, confused. Why had she come here? She turned and gazed at one of Janeway's works and remembered sticking a clay nose on a clay sculpture.

It aroused no interest, no emotion—it was an irrelevant action that—

A sudden scent, present and then gone, of rot, of carrion—

Something was wrong with this place. "There should be no walls," Seven said aloud, and immediately the walls dissolved. A soft, sweet-scented breeze caressed her face. "And the grass . . . it's not the right color, it should be pale purple." At once the grass changed color.

Seven wandered about, her words remaking the landscape into the one she had known, in which she had grown to maturity, had bonded with a lifemate and brought forth children, had blessed those children's children.

She thought of the right seat, and with a word it appeared; she changed the lump of clay to a large rectangular chunk of pale yellow stone. Simmik stone was her favorite medium. Harder than clay, softer than most stones, it seemed to respond to her touch as a lover might, coyly revealing the images it cloaked in its luminous depths.

Seven picked up a chisel. It was not quite the correct tool, but she itched to begin and it would suffice. She glanced down at her hand and gasped. The right one was a yellow-pink hue instead of her normal bright scarlet. Was she ill? And where were the calluses, the wrinkles that she had proudly put there over a lifetime of producing art and raising children? Her heart began to pound, and even it was in the wrong place—in her chest, not her belly . . .

And the left hand! Encased in a glove of metal. She flexed it. It obeyed her commands well enough . . . .

Ah, there it was. Surely it had been only her imagination, that her hands were young and had five fingers instead of the proper seven. Now those hands curled around the tools and she regarded the stone.

"A self-portrait, I think," she said aloud to hear the soft rumbling purr of her voice. "I've lived long enough. Come on, Druana. Let's see how noble those wrinkles of yours look."

She moved toward the stone, caressed it, felt the longing within it to become something Other. And then, laughter burbling on her lips, Druana began to sculpt.

CHAPTER
4

CHAKOTAY STRODE BRISKLY INTO THE TRANSPORTER room, followed by two security guards, Ramirez and Dawson. The door hissed shut behind them.

"Sir, Tamaak Vriis says the Skedans are ready to beam up," said Ensign Lyssa Campbell at the transporter console.

"Then let's get them aboard and give them a proper Starfleet welcome," he replied.

She smiled and bent her blonde head over the console, her long fingers moving with practiced speed.

Chakotay had requested, and been granted, permission to be present to welcome their passengers aboard. Janeway's effusive compliments of the Skedans in general and their leader, Tamaak Vriis, in particular had piqued his curiosity. And, not coincidentally, sent up a warning signal. Captain Janeway was unfailingly courteous and it was not unusual for her to speak highly of those who had commanded her respect. But Chakotay wanted to see for himself how "intelligent, humorous, gentle, and helpful" this little band of refugees really was.

He supposed the skepticism was the Maquis in him still, even after more than four years of wearing the Federation uniform. The thought sobered him. The Maquis were no more. Dead. Wiped out by the Cardassians, save for a handful lucky enough to be the Federation's prisoners.

The hum of the transporter snapped him out of his melancholy and he smiled despite himself as their guests took solid shape and peered about curiously.

Their large eyes, graceful movements and soft-looking fur appealed to the human affection for certain animals—deer and kangaroo came to mind. It wasn't logical. Appearance had nothing to do with the true nature of an alien, but Chakotay felt the eons-old tug nonetheless. One of them stepped forward, fixing him with those limpid eyes.

"You are Commander Chakotay?"

Chakotay was surprised. "Yes, how did you know?"

The Skedan half-closed its eyes in its equivalent of a human smile. "Lucky guess." It lifted a foreleg to its own head, protected by a ridge of bone, and tapped the fur above the eye. "Your marking, Commander."

Of course, thought Chakotay, his suspicions

quelled. *It probably came up in a conversation about rank and markings.* He recalled the name of the Skedan with whom Janeway had conversed. "And you are Tamaak Vriis?"

"Indeed I am. Commander, we are more grateful than we can say for your assistance." He hesitated, then confided, "It grows difficult to sustain hope, after so many years, but hope you have again given us that we will reach our destination. The young ones," and he gestured to several smaller Skedans, some of whom were still in their mothers' pouches, "need a home. A place to call their own. A purpose to follow."

"We'll do everything we can," Chakotay assured him. He certainly could identify with the need to put down roots. His own adolescence and youth had been turbulent, filled with a quest to find a place in the universe. Ironically, that quest for individuality, his stubborn "contrariness," had led him in a circle back to his father's teachings—the very thing he had thought he wished to escape.

He wanted to talk more with the Skedans, and would, but right now there was protocol to observe. "It is required that your people be scanned for possible weapons or anything that might pose a danger. Plus, as we are not familiar with your technology, we're going to have to do a hand search of your belongings. Please don't take offense."

"Of course not. We understand perfectly and will cooperate to the fullest extent." Tamaak gestured, and the six Skedans stepped forward, handing over their ratty packs without complaint for inspection.

"Tell me, if I am not being too forward," Tamaak

said, stepping closer to Chakotay, "what is the meaning of the mark on your face? We too have ritual markings that denote our ranks and position in society," he added, showing a circle crisscrossed with stripes on his right shoulder.

Completely comfortable with the conversation, Chakotay told Tamaak of his father's people, the meaning of the tattoo, and of the Sky Spirits who had given them so much. And as he talked, it was almost as if he were back in those days of his youth. He could have practically sworn he smelled the sweet, calming fragrance of sage, the herb his father burned in purification rituals.

Lyssa Campbell gazed at the aliens. Everyone knew how helpful they'd been in untangling some of the Lhiaarian Empire's red tape. The Skedans were also refugees. Something, she didn't know what, had happened to their homeworld and they were now seeking a new place to live. It was sad, really, especially as they seemed like such decent people.

Lyssa Campbell knew all about being ripped away from a place she loved. She had grown up on a colony that was, essentially, the frontier. When she was only eleven, her baby sister had been killed and the rest of her family had fled for their lives. Lyssa and her parents had survived, but they hadn't even had packs, like the Skedans. She wondered, as Lieutenant Ramirez and Ensign Dawson went through the shoddy packs that had clearly seen years of hard traveling, what had happened to the Skedan homeworld.

One of the younger ones met her gaze and ambled over toward her. "Hello," it said, peering up at her shyly.

"Well, hi," Lyssa smiled brightly. "What's your name, little one?"

"Thena," it said, its girlish voice a whisper. "Pretty buttons," it added, peering up at the console. "Can I touch?"

"Well, only the ones I tell you to, okay?" She glanced up, trying to find little Thena's mother. An elegant Skedan saw the two of them together and half-closed her eyes.

Permission granted to play, thought Lyssa. "Okay, up we go!" Thena chortled with delight as, held in Lyssa Campbell's encircling arms, she reached out a single digit to caress the glowing lights on the console.

Lyssa couldn't keep the smile off her face. Her baby sister, Lara, had been entranced by dancing lights as well. The warm weight she carried filled her heart, and, for just an instant, she thought she caught a whiff of apple pie—Lara's favorite.

Luis Ramirez admired the toughness of the Skedans. They'd clearly survived some dreadful ordeal, but their spirits were undaunted. In the packs he found nothing that resembled a weapon—only food-stuffs, utensils, and other harmless items. Just to be certain, he passed a tricorder over Tamaak Vriis's pack and repeated the process with the others. The tricorder registered nothing out of the ordinary. The Skedans posed no threat.

He straightened and nodded to Chakotay. Beside him, his fellow security officer, Ensign Dawson, completed his inspection of the remaining packs.

"No weapons, sir," he told the first officer.

"I'm not surprised," said Chakotay, and smiled warmly at Tamaak. "Ramirez, will you escort our guests to Cargo Bay One? I apologize for not offering you proper quarters, Tamaak, but for so many—"

Tamaak held up a placating—hand? Paw? "No need, Commander. When you have traveled as poorly and as long as we have, any place out of the wind and rain seems like a blessing from the One-Who-Makes Herself. With your permission, I will remain to greet the rest of my people."

"Certainly. Ramirez?"

Ramirez smiled at the small band. He saw the strength in their faces, the wisdom in their eyes, and was fiercely glad that Janeway had decided to lend them a hand. As he turned to lead them to Cargo Bay One, he thought he smelled the faint scent of mangos ripening on the tree.

Seven of Nine was suddenly aware of a tremendous weariness. She stumbled backward, blinking. Where was she? This was not her alcove in Cargo Bay Two. Nor was it the familiar, sterile environment of sickbay, fast becoming the place where she seemed to spend most of her time.

It had to be the holodeck. But what program? She certainly hadn't designed one, and it looked nothing like the few she had visited with Janeway or, once, with Harry Kim. The grass was purple. And before her was—

She felt a flicker of alarm. Before her was a three-meter-high carving of a female humanoid. She recognized Species 407. She fought back panic with the words that had brought comfort before: *Species 407. Advanced technology, but a race with a disproportionate interest in its culture and art rather than its science. Resistance was minimal. Their biological and technological distinctiveness . . .*

The words faded from her mind as she stared at the carving. The female was elderly. Its seven-fingered hands were gnarled, but in one she grasped a simplified image of a sun, in the other, a moon. The face showed what the humans called "character." It was strong, but soft.

Seven knew it. It was she.

"No," she whispered. She glanced down at her hands, saw the five fingers, the implants. She wasn't that woman. *Druana,* a voice said softly inside her head. And yet—

She sank down, her legs no longer supporting her, and curled up into a fetal position. The four black birds kept her company, though she did her best to ignore them.

In the course of human history, one of the things that most terrified that race was a fear of going insane. The colorful phrase that cropped up was "losing one's mind," as if a mind were something concrete that could be placed down and then forgotten. Twenty-fourth century medicine had been able to prevent or successfully treat most diseases of the brain. The dreadful threat of "insanity," laden with its primal horror, had diminished, though it was still a possibility.

As Seven went over everything that had happened to her, she could not shake the conviction that such a catastrophe was happening to her. There seemed to be no reason for her "visions." There had been no signal from the Borg, no trigger for a repressed memory. Besides, these scenarios were obviously not her own memories. They seemed to have no real connection to her; it was as if, for a brief time, she became someone else, lived their lives, enacted their dreams and fears, and channeled their creativity.

As before, her single eye welled with the wetness of tears. This alone was enough to convey to her that something powerful was occurring. Seven of Nine did not weep. She forced her hands to unclench, and with fingers that trembled so badly it took two tries, pressed her commbadge.

"Seven of Nine to Sickbay." The words rasped against her throat.

"The Doctor here. Seven, what's wrong?"

The concern in his voice brought more tears. She looked again at the sculpture, the masterful self-portrait of a self that was not her, done by hands that had no talent and no training.

"Doctor." She licked her lips, tried again. "Doctor. I think—I think I am losing my mind."

CHAPTER
5

"ALL RISE FOR HIS MOST EXCELLENT WORTHINESS, Emperor Beytek Nak-Sur the Seventh!"

The thirteen members of the Iora, the advisory council to the Emperor, dutifully got to their feet as their leader entered the ornately decorated chamber. The Iora's leader, Xanarit Ilt la, watched his compatriots carefully out of the corner of his slit-pupiled eyes. Some seemed less than impressed with their sworn leader, standing casually and not snapping promptly to attention. That was unacceptable.

Beytek entered in his customary manner: borne on a litter carried by four sturdy Imperial guards. Xanarit stiffened. This was an ancient custom recently revived by the young Emperor, and no one save Beytek himself particularly liked it. But the whims of a ruler of ninety-six worlds—ninety-seven not so long ago, but Xanarit wasn't even supposed to think about that—were as rigid as law.

The faces of the noble guards who carried him, rulers of their own powerful Houses, were expressionless. Their eyesacs were a neutral shade of purple, revealing nothing. Xanarit allowed his thin lips to curve in a slight, sardonic smile. One who served the Emperor learned the skill of cloaking emotions early on. But Xanarit knew that beneath the calm exterior of the guards' face-scales, anger burned at a fever pitch. It was an honor to guard the Emperor, to offer one's life in service, to perhaps sacrifice that life in battle or in protecting the man who was incarnation of the Empire.

But to carry around a young man with two perfectly serviceable legs? That bordered on insult.

At least, Xanarit thought, Beytek had left the entourage of musicians back at the pleasure-room. That was something.

Beytek lounged on the litter, waving a small fan of rare *kunnagit* feathers. The room was climate controlled, set constantly at the precise temperature the Lhiaarians preferred. The air circulated freely for peak comfort. Beytek didn't need a fan to cool his blue-scaled face any more than he needed four large men to carry him, but it was part of the image he wanted to cultivate. Languidly, he reached down with the feathered fan and stroked the neck of the man bearing the back left portion of the litter. The guard flinched at the tickling brush of the feathers, and his pupils briefly dilated in a flash of anger that was immediately quelled.

"Down," barked the guard to his three comrades, and the Emperor's litter was lowered to the thick, soft carpet. Beytek stepped off and smiled at his guards. His black tongue flicked out, scenting the air. He waved a clawed hand.

"Dismissed," he said airily, then went to his cushion on the highest tier and curled up happily on it. The thirteen members of the Iora waited patiently for instructions that they might sit on their own cushions, positioned a respectful two tiers below that of their emperor. Languidly, Beytek hummed to himself as he examined a plateful of treats and selected the choicest delicacies. Only after he had eaten three juicy *tii* fruits and washed them down with a bowl of expensive *voor* wine did he flick his tail and order, "You may be seated."

Xanarit regarded his master—his god, according to religious tradition—with contempt. The Nak-Sur dynasty was an old and noble one. Xanarit himself had served loyally and happily under Beytek the Sixth, an intelligent, humorous, and noble leader. Nearly a third of the present Empire was acquired under Beytek the Sixth's reign, and following the tradition of naming each emperor's reign, the late ruler's had been officially dubbed "The Peaceful and Profitable Reign of the Sky-Lord Joy-Bringer."

Idly, Xanarit wondered how history would remember Beytek the Seventh. "The Squandered and Wasteful Reign of Pleasure-Loving Shame-Maker," perhaps? Or maybe "The Devastating and Frightening Reign of Non-Listening Division-Bringer."

Xanarit caught the eye of his Second, Mintik. She held his gaze a moment, then returned her attention to the slothful excuse for a leader who commanded their attention. Everyone present hated the emperor. But at the moment, it would mean their lives and that of their whole families, down to the smallest child, to admit it.

"With your permission, O Great One?" Xanarit asked in a humble voice. Pleased at the servile tone, Beytek nodded his head that the head of his Iora might proceed. "It pains me more than words can say to bring this news, but there is trouble brewing in the world of Tatori."

Beytek crunched another bite of food. "Where's that?"

Only years of practice kept Xanarit's face from betraying him. "On the outskirts of our Empire, Sector 408. Elebon Boma, the Tatori ruler, has sent a fifth petition requesting food and a means by which to extract water from the atmosphere. Medical supplies—"

"Would be wasted on those pathetic things," drawled Beytek. "As I recall, they didn't even make proper tribute last year. Will there be a representative from Tatori this year?"

Tribute, a yearly ritual on Lhiaari, was only a few days away. Each year, a representative from each world brought the amount of tribute his or her world owed the Empire for protection, sustenance, and inclusion. Some gave food or precious minerals. Others just gave money. Some donated slave labor. A few enterprising worlds had offered exclusive rights to new technologies they had developed.

Xanarit hesitated a moment before replying. "No, O Great One. They have nothing to give. Had we supplied them with the equipment they requested, which was promised to them in the Treaty of Minaa, which your father signed, they would have been able to irrigate their crops and—"

"My father signed it," retorted Beytek, his eyesacs changing color with his anger. "I did not! Why should we waste precious technology on such a backward planet? Let them develop their own equipment, I say. Hrrrk!" He shuddered in irritation and calmed himself by popping a ripe berry into his mouth.

"O Great One," said Xanarit in a deceptively soft voice, "if you persist in not honoring treaties, you will cause unrest among your peoples. It is a little thing, this device that is due the Tatori, and it could save millions of lives. Think of the honor that would be due you! Think how the name of Beytek the Seventh will ring upon the tongues of the grateful Tatori!"

For a moment, it appeared as if that argument might sway the young ruler. He paused and inflated his chin-sacks with pleasure. Then he shook his head and drank some more wine.

"No. There's no point in it."

Xanarit felt a knot growing in the pit of his second stomach. *No point in it.* No point in dispatching some of the most common, least expensive Lhiaarian technology to a dying planet that needed only water to revive. It took all the control that the chief advisor could summon not to launch himself up at the raised tier upon which the Emperor lounged and rip the arrogant youngling's soft throat out, but that would accomplish nothing.

No point in it.

Instead, Xanarit obsequiously ducked his head. "As my most honored ruler wishes." He turned to examine the next issue on the list, but Beytek surprised him by initiating another subject.

"I've heard a rumor—unconfirmed, of course— that the Skedans have been seen on one of the Imperial waystations." He leaned forward and flicked his tongue. "Have you heard about this rumor, Xanarit?" His eyes darted about. "Any of you?"

Murmurs of protest rose from the assembled Council. Xanarit had to call upon his deep powers of concentration to prevent his eyesacs from turning red and thus betraying his emotions. "Who is spreading such distressing falsehoods?"

Beytek's smile grew and he shrugged. "Rumors are like the tariflies, they buzz about with no clear point of origin."

By the Great Father, he's got the Ku out looking for them! Beytek was hardly a master of deceit, and even when he was trying to be cryptic, he often—as he just had—betrayed himself. Xanarit loathed the Ku for a variety of reasons, but mostly for the pleasure they took in their job. Killing for a ruler was nothing new, and in fact was an honorable profession. But there was a world—an empire—of difference between honorable warfare and the stealth of the assassin, the flash of the sword of antiquity or the energy weapon of today versus the knife to the throat in the night. No one was supposed to know about the Ku, but everyone did. But they were not spoken of. Not here, not ever, save in hushed whispers.

Because the Emperor could turn the Ku on anyone.

Beytek was staring at Xanarit expectantly, and the chief advisor searched for words. "Then perhaps the buzzing of these rumors should be regarded as merely an annoyance, as we regard the tariflies."

"Perhaps they shouldn't."

"Very well, then let us assume there are a few Skedans who have somehow survived, escaped the Borg, left their quarantined planet, and found a way to get this close to Lhiaari without being detected." Xanarit's voice dripped scorn. "Then, my master, you should perhaps spend a season gambling on the Shamrik Moon—the odds are about as good."

"Do you think I'm a fool, Xanarit?" yelped the Emperor. "I know what I'm saying, and I'm saying there are Skedans within the borders of my empire! I want you to double security on every waystation. And I want to know every last detail about this year's Tribute celebration. If a rodent eats grain at a storage facility, I want to know about it. Do you hear me?"

"I hear and obey, O Great One." Xanarit let it hang in the air between them for a moment, then dipped his head to look at the list. "We now must discuss—"

"Nothing!" A fine tantrum was building, Xanarit

could see that. Growling, Beytek seized the tray and hurled it at Xanarit. Gracefully, the chief advisor ducked, which seemed to enrage Beytek all the more. "We will discuss nothing but what I say we discuss! Don't you understand? If there are Skedans alive, and they are heading this way, everything will be ruined! Everything! And if I fall, I swear this to you, each of you will fall with me. So you'd better listen to the tariflies, my so-called advisory council. Listen and when next I summon you, you had better have some advice worth listening to!"

He stormed out, shunning the litter bearers who abruptly snapped to attention. The four guards exchanged glances, then hastened after their wrathful lord.

Xanarit watched them go in silence. When he was certain they were truly alone, he turned to the others.

"How long would it be before we can arrange to have a water-extraction system smuggled to Tatori?"

He listened as the rest of the council discussed the matter and focused more on the fact that he was saving innocent lives than that he was committing the ultimate sin for a Lhiaarian—treason.

"How are you feeling?" Captain Janeway's voice was soft, warm with concern, and her forehead was furrowed.

What a foolish question. Typical of a human.

"I am not well," replied Seven. Surely it was obvious. She was lying down in the diagnostic bed. The Doctor had taken several samples of just about everything in Seven's body, including her nanites. He had run over a dozen tests. She was frightened, exhausted, weak.

And the five black birds persisted in accompanying her.

Something suddenly broke in her and she screamed at them, "Go away! Leave me alone!" She tried to bolt upright but the diagnostic bed constrained her. The Doctor was there at once, trying to calm her down.

"Seven! It's all right! There's no one here to hurt you!"

But she didn't hear him, didn't hear Janeway and her efforts to soothe. All she could hear was the soft cawing of the birds, the birds who wouldn't let her be—

Suddenly Seven ceased struggling and simply stared at them. She felt the strong hands of the Doctor on her shoulders, pressing her back down. She resisted, locking eyes with each of the birds—ravens—in turn.

They weren't the enemy. They were the one constant in Seven's abruptly shifting universe. She didn't know why she was wafting in and out of other people's lives in this frightening way. For so long, Seven of Nine had been a part of the collective, part of a vast, intricate network that had no place for individuality. Now, faced with losing the individuality that had been so abruptly foisted upon her, Seven realized she wanted to keep it. And somehow, in a way that she didn't understand, these ravens were the key to holding on to who she was.

Something about their song.

No, not *their* song—

She turned wide eyes to the Doctor. "It's the ravens," she said. "They're—"

But the Doctor pressed something metallic and cold to the base of her head. Seven heard a soft hissing, thought frantically, *No! I have almost grasped it . . . .*

Then she knew no more.

CHAPTER
6

"I THINK THEY'RE AWFULLY NICE," SAID PARIS, TAPPING the bright keys on the console. "Especially the kids. One of the older ones—Priana, I think her name is— she's adorable. And real smart. We were walking through the corridor yesterday en route to the holo- deck and she wanted to know—"

"Can't anyone talk about anything but the Ske- dans?" snapped Torres.

Paris shot her a look. "A little touchy, aren't we?"

"I don't think so. They've been on board for three days now and no one can seem to come up with anything to talk about but them, how nice they are, how smart, how this, how that. Frankly, it's beginning to disgust me."

"Okay, okay," said Paris, fighting back a sudden burst of irritation. Something had been bothering B'Elanna ever since the aliens came on board. She had seemed to take an instant dislike to them, especially the bright little female called Priana whom Tom had "adopted" for the duration of the stay. Tom couldn't figure it out. Admittedly, Torres didn't have the normal human tendency to get all mushy over cute kids, but she usually respected others unless they had done something of which she disapproved. And to the best of his knowledge, the refugees had done nothing except save the *Voyager* crew time and trouble. Priana was a sharp cookie, chock-full of questions and a lot of fun to be around. What was Torres's problem?

Whatever was bugging her extended to Tom. He hadn't been able to so much as put an arm around her recently. Anything more was out of the question, but she wouldn't give him a good answer as to why. After all they'd been through together—all he thought they'd meant to each other—Tom thought he at least deserved an explanation. Instead, all he got were more blasts of Torres temper. Too bad they couldn't bottle her vitriol—it'd make a hell of a weapon.

The warp drive was back on line. Captain Janeway had told him to spend the full shift working down here in Engineering if he needed it. Normally he'd take advantage of the opportunity to be with B'Elanna. Now, though, just being around her exasperated him. He couldn't get away fast enough.

"Problem solved," he said brusquely. "See you later." Without another word he strode out of Engineering, refusing to feel any sort of guilt even though he felt B'Elanna's gaze boring into his back.

As the door hissed open, he heard Vorik's calm voice stating, "To their credit, the Skedans are extremely logical." Paris smothered a grin. The door closed before he could hear B'Elanna's outraged retort.

Paris found that he wasn't returning to the bridge as he had planned. Instead, he was heading toward Cargo Bay One. His heart felt lighter with each step. The captain wasn't expecting him back on the bridge for the rest of his shift. And he wasn't exactly ducking his duty, was he? Surely Captain Janeway would encourage her crew to be accessible to their guests, the ones responsible for their speedy passage.

The door hissed open. And as if she had been expecting him, little Priana was right by the door. Her large, soft eyes lit up.

"Tom!" she said, half-closing those eyes in a gesture of pleasure. "I am so pleased to see you!"

He felt the smile spreading across his face. Already the tense afternoon spent sniping at B'Elanna was fading from his memory. "I have a little bit of free time. If you'd like, we could finish our tour."

"I would enjoy that very much." Playfully, Tom bowed and extended his arm. Shyly, Priana looped her own arm through it and laughed. Her voice was melodious, soft—even her fur was soft and yielding. Not words one would apply to B'Elanna Torres. Priana was, overall, much better company than the fiery half-Klingon, and as they walked down the corridors chatting amiably, Paris thought that this was a much better way to spend a free afternoon.

As they strolled arm in arm toward the turbolift, Paris felt more at peace than he had been since his last camping trip. The feeling was so profound that he almost could smell the comforting, cool scent of pine.

Seven blinked. Her right eye was filled with some sort of crusty, gritty material and she brushed at it absently.

"Humans call it sleep sand," said the Doctor, noticing her movements. "There are all kinds of stories told to children about the Sandman sprinkling the stuff in one's eyes with the purpose of bringing restful sleep. Similar to the legends of the Tooth Fairy. Personally, I find the thought of some spirit or magical being hovering about a child as it sleeps and pouring sand into its eyes rather disturbing, but it seems to calm the humans."

"But it is not sand at all," said Seven, frowning. "It is merely the encrusted—"

"You're missing the point," said the Doctor irritably. She looked up at him. "Seven, you slept. For ten hours, I might add. That's a first for you."

"You injected me with a hypospray."

"Which wore off after approximately twenty minutes. You were sleeping quite naturally and very soundly." He glanced up from arranging his tools on a tray and grinned. "Snoring, as a matter of fact." At her look, he added, "Quite audibly."

Seven frowned. "I do not snore."

"How would you know?"

He had an excellent point and she decided not to pursue it. Of more immediate concern were the strange images that she recalled—fragmented, bizarre visions.

"Doctor, I believe I dreamed. It was—most unusual. The images that I saw seemed disjointed."

"Again—perfectly normal for humans, or so I understand. Dreams are images from the subconscious. The mind is working on finding solutions and uses dreams to do so. Sometimes the meaning of a dream is obvious. More often, the brain uses metaphors."

"They were most illogical."

"I'm sure they were." He bent and ran the tricorder over her. "Were any of your dreams about these other lives?"

She shook her head. "No."

"How about your feathered friends?"

For an instant, Seven thought—hoped—they had gone. Perhaps this sleep had banished them. But upon looking around sickbay, she saw them—six of them, now—clustered in a corner. All of them were staring at her.

"The birds are still present, Doctor."

"And your limbic system is active." He snapped shut the tricorder. "Seven, we've discussed this before, but—do these birds have any sort of meaning for you? Something that might have been in your dreams, perhaps?"

Seven thought about her dreams for a moment before replying. "There was one in which I was supposed to report to Astrometrics. Captain Janeway was there, and Chakotay—all the senior staff. I had designed a very important program. But when I had to demonstrate it—" She turned her eyes on the Doctor. "—I had forgotten everything. Everything!"

"That's a version of a very common dream," he reassured her. "The ones I usually hear about concern failing Starfleet Academy exams."

"And there was one where I was falling—and one where I realized I was unclothed, but I was on the bridge and—"

"All normal dreams," said the Doctor. Seven thought he looked a bit uncomfortable and wondered if he had always been programmed to blush or if that was a new subroutine. "I'm afraid that figuring this out is all up to you. Dreams are tailored to the individual—there's not usually a common language, so to speak. Try to look for a pattern in these recurring hallucinations. Think about what ravens mean to you. You say that's the one constant."

One of the ravens pecked at another, which cawed and flew to a safer perch. "That is correct."

"And they do not appear when you have the hallucinations."

"No, they do not."

"I think these birds are your subconscious. Like your dreams. They—"

"Yes," breathed Seven, remembering the faintest echo of the revelation that had broken over her before the Doctor had sedated her. "Yes . . . I almost had it. Something about . . . about their song . . . ."

"I'm a doctor, not an ornithologist, but to the best

of my recollection, ravens don't have a particularly appealing song."

Seven was nodding, staring at the six birds. Six. That number was important too. "Not their song. A song about them. An old song . . . a song I know."

"Perhaps one of your ditties from your trip to twentieth-century France?" Seven's holodeck stint as a cabaret singer when the ship was under the command of the Hirogen was something of a legend on *Voyager*. The role had been so out of character for her, it had made more of an impression on the crew than Tuvok's bartender or Chakotay's American soldier. No one had expected Seven, with her clipped, precise manner of speaking, to be able to belt out a song quite so skillfully. She glared at him.

"No. There were no bird songs in that hologram's repertoire. The song must therefore be something that I learned as a child. Doctor, am I well enough to return to duty?"

"Definitely not." His tone brooked no argument. "There's no warning before these hallucinations of yours. So far, you've confined yourself to hunting birds and sculpting a statue. But suppose you were to leap into the life of a warrior and destroy the ship?"

Seven was startled at how upset she was becoming and made an attempt to calm herself. Railing at the Doctor would accomplish nothing.

"I believe that you are correct. These birds and this song will help me better understand what is transpiring. However, I will need to access the computer and determine what song it might be. I will not attempt to—"

"Not by yourself. Sickbay to bridge."

"Janeway here."

"Sleeping Beauty has just awoken and wishes to access the computer. I don't dare let her do so alone. Is there someone available who could assist her?"

"I'll put Harry on it."

"Ah, Mr. Kim. An excellent choice. Sickbay out." He turned to Seven. "May I make a suggestion?"

"Certainly."

"You might not wish to go into details with Ensign Kim about your dreams."

Humor, thought Seven. She relaxed a little under the Doctor's slight smile, and curved her full lips in one of her own.

Seven was shocked and rather dismayed to find out how many Earth-based songs concerned birds. *A Bird in a Guilded Cage. Birds Do It, Bees Do It. Listen to the Mockingbird. Freebird. When the Red Red Robin Comes Bob-Bob-Bobbin' Along.* One song, called a Christmas carol, mentioned a variety of fowl including swans, partridges, geese, turtledoves, and some unidentifiable species known as "calling birds" and "French hens." None of the titles meant anything to her, so they had to play excerpts. The sound of the computer issuing music and vocals in the sterile environment of Astrometrics made for a peculiar contrast of which even Seven was aware.

"This is not a place for—for popular songs," she said in a disapproving tone. The computer cheerfully belted out a song in which all the little birds went tweet, tweet, tweet. Seven found it annoying in a manner she could not articulate.

"Hey, this was your idea," said Harry.

"Lieutenant Torres once told me that you have a fondness for a special type of Earth-based story-telling format specifically geared toward entertaining your young called nursery rhymes."

Kim rolled his eyes and fiddled with the computer. Another song issued forth. "Thanks, B'Elanna," he muttered under his breath.

"Once, she said that your knowledge proved useful in a fact-finding mission called . . ." She furrowed her brow as she tried to recall the term. "Brainstorming?"

"Yeah. So you want me to brainstorm about birds?"

"You are angry," Seven stated. "I am uncertain as to why. Do you not wish to assist me in determining what is causing my hallucinations?"

"No, of course I do, but—okay." He took a deep breath. "Ravens or some other black bird, huh?"

"Correct."

Kim cocked his head and thought. "Edgar Allan Poe. Nevermore. *The Twa Corbies. Sing a Song of Sixpence.* The Ugly Duckling. No, wait, he turned into a swan. Umm . . . ."

But Seven had gone cold inside. The birds had suddenly erupted into a chorus of shrieking. They were flying about, their wings flapping, hugely excited.

Yes. *Sing a song of sixpence, a pocket full of rye; four and twenty blackbirds—*

Pain ripped through her, exquisite in its agony.

That awful smell of carrion filled her nostrils and twisted her stomach into knots. Her knees buckled and with a low groan she collapsed. Harry seized her elbows and tried to lift her. She heard his voice, but faintly, as if he were far away: "Seven? Seven, are you all right?"

Why was he calling her Seven? She was the First of Six in her household—that was, until the Great Destroyers came. And his face—hideous! Deformed! Frantically, Amari seized his face and cried out, "What have the Destroyers done to you? Oh, my love, my love . . . ." She kissed him, and when she pulled back Sulmi's face was again the handsome, feathered visage she so adored. His expression was confused, and the words he spoke were curious:

"Doctor, I'm bringing Seven in right now. It's happening again."

CHAPTER 7

CAPTAIN'S LOG, SUPPLEMENTAL. SEVEN OF NINE IS BACK
in sickbay. The Doctor is concerned and, frankly, so
am I. Seven has become a valuable member of this
crew, and despite our clashes, a friend as well. Try as I
might, I can't envision journeying without her.

Her condition is currently stable, but erratic overall.
Presently she is unconscious, but I can't think of safer
hands for anyone than the Doctor's. Despite my personal concern, we need to press on.

We are approaching the second required waystation
in Imperial space and are preparing to rendezvous with
its stationmaster. There are three more waystations
before we reach the Lhiaarian homeworld. I couldn't

imagine negotiating the forty-three that would be required without permission from the Emperor. Let's hope that when we finally have an audience with Emperor Beytek, he's in a good mood.

"Status report?" Janeway asked as she strode briskly onto the bridge from her ready room.

"We have just been contacted by Stationmaster Vooria's vessel," Ensign Kim informed her. "She's requesting permission to come aboard."

"Permission granted—gratefully," added the captain as she slipped into her command chair. "Janeway to Tamaak Vriis." Silence. She exchanged glances with Chakotay, whose confused expression indicated that he didn't know why the leader of the Skedans did not respond either.

"Janeway to Tamaak Vriis, please respond."

There was another pause, then finally: "Tamaak Vriis here, Captain."

"Stationmaster Vooria is preparing to beam aboard. I'm sending someone to escort you to the conference room immediately."

"Captain—I am terribly sorry about this, but—we are in the midst of performing a very meaningful ritual. We need to complete it. May I respectfully request that we postpone this meeting?"

"Tamaak," said Chakotay, "You know I understand how important such rituals are to your people. But this meeting is important, too. It's taken hours just to get a Lhiaarian representative to agree to see us, and we need your special brand of diplomacy if we want to get to the Emperor."

A pause. "Just a few minutes, Captain. I beg you."

"Captain, if I may make a suggestion," said Tuvok. "We hope to convince the Lhiaarian stationmaster to report favorably to her emperor. A brief tour of *Voyager* might intrigue her sufficiently and influence the tenor of her report. We are, after all, attempting to persuade Emperor Beytek that we are worth an audience."

"Excellent idea, Tuvok," approved Janeway. "Tamaak, you've got a half-hour. Not a minute more. Understood?"

"Completely, Captain. And I thank you."

Tamaak Vriis turned off the communicator and regarded his people. They were all together, standing quietly in a circle. Their concentration had been broken, but not shattered by the interruption. They could easily link again and complete the ritual.

He took a deep, calming breath, and reached out to touch the minds of all that remained of the Skedan race. The strong, cold thoughts of Imraak. The light, gentle brush of Shemaak's mind. The fire and passion of the lovely Priana, raised to an almost unbearable heat by her attraction to this vessel's pilot. Little Thena and her dam, all of them, joined as one in this moment to nurture the single thing that meant more to the Skedans than anything else in the galaxy, including the survival of their species.

Revenge.

The incongruously beautiful weapon which would execute the ultimate goal of the surviving Skedans sat in a place of honor in the center of their circle.

Carefully cradled on a soft purple cushion, the weapon was a small sphere. Not quite small enough to fit in a single paw, but certainly much smaller than little Thena.

Gently, compassionately, Tamaak reached out with his mental powers and touched each mind individually. Like a weaver pulling the individual threads into a glorious whole, he gathered thought, knowledge, and emotion until they were of one mind, one heart, one soul.

He turned his large eyes toward the Sphere and directed their thoughts toward it. They wrapped it in an invisible blanket of love and protection. Earlier, when they had first come aboard *Voyager*, careless human hands had passed analyzing equipment over the Sphere. Their tricorders, as the tools were called, beeped a shrill warning at the high level of unidentifiable energy radiating from the Sphere.

But Ramirez, wrapped in his warrior's regard for the Skedans as fellow survivors, his nostrils filled with the sweet scent of mangoes from his native Earth, had noticed nothing. Nor had Dawson, distracted in a fashion tailored just for him; nor Chakotay, enthralled by the markings he "saw" on Tamaak's naked arm. Even Thena, small as she was, had kept the faith and purpose of the Skedans true by playing on Lyssa Campbell's longing for a baby sister.

Ease itself it was to fool these humans, to make them see what the Skedans wished them to see, to trick them into trusting their eyes and ears even when their equipment clearly registered something else.

Surely the arrival of these *Voyagers* was a direct blessing, a gift from She-Who-Makes to let them know that She approved of their purpose.

There had only been one who knew of their power, who might have stopped them, but she was being dealt with. And that, too, had been a joyful exercise.

Part of Tamaak regretted fooling these intelligent, caring people. He liked them. Their minds were full of the most interesting images. He would have liked to meet them under better, different circumstances. He would have liked to have honest discourse, fair trade.

But the death of their world had obliterated more than the Borg could ever have anticipated. Along with the millions of dead and assimilated, the Borg left a handful of people who had suddenly learned how to hate. When there was no thought of a crop to tend, or a family to love, or even a legacy to leave, the burning desire for justice, for revenge, rushed to fill that aching void.

Before Tamaak, the Sphere seemed to shimmer. Its wards had been refreshed, renewed for the day. No mind on this vessel could detect its true nature. No weapon could damage it. It—and their one last hope— was utterly safe.

Tamaak let out a deep sigh. All around him, his kin shook their heads, flexed muscles that had been held a bit too tautly. It was done. The rite had ended.

And just in time, too. The door hissed open and Tom Paris stood there, smiling. His blue eyes sought out Priana's, and the smile widened.

"Hi," he said softly. She lowered her eyes lest he

know just how happy she was to see him. "Tamaak, I'm to escort you to the conference room."

The scream that tore Seven's throat brought her awake. The Doctor was there at once.

"Seven?" It was a question, uttered in a hesitant voice. She licked her lips, tasting the salty tang of sweat on them. Her whole face felt damp with moisture. She disliked the sensation intensely. The Borg did not sweat.

"Yes, it is I." Peculiar word, that. One letter in the English alphabet, and yet it meant so much—more than her mind had even been truly able to grasp, yet. *I. Me. Myself.* The question of identity, of individuality, of a singular, unique entity dreadfully alone in the universe.

"Thank heavens for that." She felt cold metal against her neck and heard the hiss of the hypospray. Her rapid heartbeat slowed and she felt calmer. "Since Ensign Kim brought you in to sickbay this afternoon," the Doctor continued, "I've had to deal with Druana, Keela, Amari, To-Do-Ka, Shrri, and Zarmuk the Father-Warrior. You make a very interesting male, Seven."

He ran the tricorder over her and frowned. "Your body has been running on the contents of my hypospray for far too long. You need to regenerate and eat something."

Seven wasn't paying attention. She stared at the seven black birds who kept her silent company. *I remembered the rhyme you were trying to tell me about,* she thought to them, knowing that they could hear her. Foolish, to direct a thought to a hallucination. But these birds—these birds with their ever increasing numbers and reassuring if illusory solidity—were her lifeline. They held the key, and part of that key was the nursery rhyme.

She took a deep breath and reached for the Doctor's hand. Surprised by the gesture, he did not pull away. He, too, was an illusion after a fashion—a hologram, not flesh and blood or machine. But he was also real, solid to the touch, and she gripped his hand hard.

"Sing a song of sixpence," she said in a flat voice, fighting for control. The Doctor's eyebrows climbed for his hairline—quite a reach—and he opened his mouth as if about to say something. She shot him a quick glance and he fell silent, sensing how important this was to her even if he couldn't understand why.

"A pocket full of rye, four and twenty blackbirds baked in a pie. When the pie was opened—"

—the birds began to sing—

And they did, in their own way, flapping about and shrieking. Seven winced at the volume; the sound hurt her ears. She still had difficulty believing that what was so clearly visible to her should be unseen by any others.

At that moment, the ship was rocked by an enormous blast. Seven gasped. Her eyes rolled back into her head. One of the birds lit on her shoulder and pecked at her ear, trying desperately to keep her here, inside her body. But the by-now familiar stench filled her nostrils and her mind.

The gleaming metal! The strange, ugly being—not the Great Destroyers, certainly, but perhaps one of their

*minions. Amari's own body was as ugly as this
being's—bipedal, naked, no colorful feathers nor elegant claws. What new, monstrous experiment was
this?*

*"Seven?" asked the being. She summoned up what
moisture she could from her terror-dried mouth and
spat at him.*

*"Ah," said the being, wiping the offensive spittle
away, "Not Seven."*

"Janeway to bridge. What's going on, Chakotay?"

Janeway knew her voice sounded strained, but the
sudden rocking of the vessel had taken her utterly by
surprise. She, Neelix, Tuvok, and Tamaak were awaiting the arrival of the Lhiaarian official in the transporter room.

"We're under attack."

"By the Lhiaarian vessel?" She glanced, shocked, at
Neelix. He looked stunned. He shook his head and
shrugged in a gesture of incomprehension. There had
been absolutely no indication of hostility in the
tedious negotiations they had just concluded. Something as alive and vital as hostility would, frankly,
have been welcomed compared to the dry discussions
in which the Lhiaarians seemed to so enjoy indulging.

"Negative. Vessel unknown."

"On my way."

She arrived on the bridge in less than three minutes.
Chakotay yielded the chair and updated her. "We'd
hoped that Vooria might be able to tell us about this
new vessel, but we've lost all contact with the stationmaster's ship. She refuses to respond to our hails."

"To hell with the stationmaster," snapped the captain, settling into her chair. "I want to know who's firing on us without provocation."

"I think you're about to find out," said Kim, glancing up from his console with an anxious look on his handsome face. "We're being hailed."

"Onscreen." Janeway took a deep, calming breath, but her eyes still snapped fire.

The breath caught in her throat. Before her on the screen was a giant insect. Its multifaceted eyes glittered and its mandibles clicked open and closed. It wore no clothing—with a strong exoskeleton it needed no such artificial protection from the elements—but there were bright splashes of paint on its body.

Janeway suppressed a deeply bred shudder of revulsion. These weren't bugs, they were people. She had to make sure she remembered that.

"I'm Captain Kathryn Janeway, of the Federation starship *Voyager*. Who are you and why have you fired on my vessel?"

The creature's antennae waved and its black, spine-covered legs moved. Its mandibles clicked rapidly. The computer translated its voice as best it could, rendering it flat and mechanical-sounding:

"I am Kraa T'Krr, and I have come for the Skedans."

CHAPTER

8

"On whose authority?" demanded Janeway. She narrowed her eyes and stuck her chin out defiantly.

"That does not concern you," came the metallic-sounding reply.

"Oh, but I think it does." Her voice was deceptively mild. Inside, she was furious. "You open fire on my ship, you demand our passengers, and you won't even tell me who wants them or why?"

"Precisely."

She turned to Kim and raised an eyebrow. The years spent serving with his captain were not wasted; Janeway knew her young ensign knew every expression that flitted across her face when she was on the bridge. He got the message, ran his fingers over the console and said, "Audio silenced."

"Keep trying to raise the stationmaster, but do so unobtrusively. I want to know what she knows about this. We could have walked unwittingly into a dispute of some kind." He nodded and restored audio.

"I'm a reasonable person. Let's discuss this. Have the Skedans committed any crime?" Janeway continued.

Kraa's antennae waved furiously. He turned and gestured with a long black foreleg to someone off-screen. The screen went blank, revealing only the ominous little ship floating against a field of bright stars.

"They're firing," said Tuvok. The shields were already up so his captain merely nodded. The blast rocked the vessel.

"Damage report?"

"Shields down ten percent. Minor injuries reported from decks seven and fourteen," replied Tuvok.

"Hail the alien vessel," Janeway snapped. "When I talk, I want him listening."

"Channel open, Captain."

"Kraa, you are doing nothing to convince me to turn over my friends and everything to convince me we should attack you in turn. Either you give me a good reason to—"

"Firing again." Tuvok's voice was calm, as ever.

"That does it," muttered Janeway. "You want a fight, we'll give you one. Red alert! Battle stations!" Immediately, the bridge darkened and a crimson glow replaced the normal lighting. "Tuvok, target their engines and weapons systems and fire at will. Harry, get me Stationmaster Vooria *now*. There's obviously been some sort of mistake. I don't like mistakes, especially when they mean my ship's in danger."

She sat erect in her chair, watching with grim determination as Tuvok fired. Red phaser energy screamed across space, striking its target but doing little damage. The ship, oval and as black and shiny as its occupants, executed a smooth roll and came back firing.

"Shields down seventeen percent," droned Tuvok. "Minor damage to the port nacelle."

"Harry—"

"Onscreen," replied the ensign. At once, the Lhiaarian official with whom they had planned to meet just a few short minutes ago appeared on the screen.

As good servants of the empire, each planet tended to use its own indigenous populace as stationmasters, military or police, and in the other myriad offices required by the bureaucratic Empire. But this woman was a true Lhiaarian. Her race was reptilian, with slitted eyes and a forked tongue that occasionally crept out to scent the air in a habit that was eons old. They were bipedal, with a long, counterbalancing tail. Perhaps most interesting were their faces—covered with small blue scales with sacs around their eyes that revealed their emotions.

That's handy for negotiating, thought Janeway. *Especially for someone who's a petty bureaucrat, tucked away here on the fringe of the Empire.*

"Stationmaster Vooria," said Janeway, fighting to keep her voice calm and diplomatic. "I'm hoping you could tell me who has decided to interrupt our important negotiations by firing without cause on my vessel."

Vooria's eyesacs were bright crimson. For an instant, Janeway thought the Lhiaarian merely annoyed, but the minute Vooria spoke Janeway realized that the stationmaster was terrified.

"Whatever it is they want," Vooria said in a voice that quivered, "do it. Immediately."

"Why?" demanded Janeway, rising and striding down toward the viewscreen.

"That does not concern you." Stationmaster Vooria's efforts to sublimate her terror only made her fear that much more obvious.

"Phrase of the day," muttered Paris.

Janeway was furious, but she continued to smile. Their enemy fired again. She stumbled but recovered her balance almost immediately.

"The attacking vessel has demanded we turn over the Skedans. Tamaak Vriis and his people came to us for aid, and in turn they have helped us. They've been the perfect guests and have harmed no one on this vessel. That's more than I can say for you or the people who are attacking us." The smile, soft and gentle, vanished. "They remain here."

"If you wish to survive," said Vooria in that same strained, choked voice, "do what they say. Then get out of Imperial space. Or stay here and die. Either way, we will have nothing more to do with you."

Vooria reached out a clawed hand and slammed it down on the panel in front of her.

Janeway was surprised by the depth of her anger.

She thought of Tamaak, of the friendliness of his people, of the endearing faces of the young ones. Turn them over to those oversized bugs for who knew what reason? Not while she still had breath in her body.

"Shields down thirty percent," said Chakotay. "Our phasers appear to be inflicting only minimal damage."

The point was illustrated an instant later when *Voyager* fired on her opponent, struck dead on, and the ship veered off in an arrogant, elegant swoop. It circled back and charged, its weapons firing. The pulsing red light flickered for an instant, then the emergency lighting went on.

"Captain," Torres called from Engineering. "That last one almost knocked the warp engines off-line. What's going on up there?"

"Captain," said Chakotay, "we're no longer welcome here by either party. I suggest we—"

"Get the hell out of Dodge," Janeway finished grimly. "I think you're right. B'Elanna, keep those engines on-line—I'll be asking for warp eight, bearing eight-five-seven-two. Tom, do it."

"Yes ma'am," replied Paris immediately. At once the ship executed a roll and then leaped into warp.

Mentally, Janeway reviewed their situation. It wasn't good. They were on the run now, with two sets of enemies behind them and no explanation as to why. At this bearing, they were making a beeline for the next closest Lhiaarian waystation. If *Voyager* could get there ahead of her pursuers, she might have a chance of figuring out what exactly was going on.

Janeway glanced over at Chakotay and smiled a little. "This feel a bit familiar?"

"Just like old times," he smiled back at her.

The captain thumbed a button. "This is Captain Janeway to all crew members. We have encountered hostility at this waystation and are presently on course to the next one in an attempt to straighten out a misunderstanding. We'll proceed at warp eight, under yellow alert. Stay on your toes, everyone."

"Sickbay to bridge."

"Bridge here," replied Janeway, rubbing her eyes.

"Can you spare Mr. Paris? I could use some help down here. What happened, anyway?"

"We just engaged in battle with an unknown adversary with an unknown grudge."

The Doctor's voice was grim when he replied. "Well, there's a battle going on here, too, and I'm afraid Seven isn't winning it."

Sickbay was full of wounded and Paris had equipment placed in his hands the minute he entered. Most of the injuries were superficial and easily treated. But in the meantime Paris knew his crewmates' wounds hurt like a sonofagun, and he immediately began running the tricorder over the nearest casualty.

Out of the corner of his eye, he saw Seven lying motionless on the diagnostic bed. Her condition seemed stable, but he could tell by the fact that the Doctor, too, stole a glance over at her from time to time that she was in trouble. She seemed so small, lying on that bed. Her bright eyes were closed and couldn't pierce him with disdain. Her full, red lips were gray and slack, slightly parted; no acerbic comment would come from them any time soon. Even her well-toned and technologically augmented body seemed frail to his eyes.

He'd heard, as all of them had at the morning briefings, that Seven was having hallucinations. Harry had turned pink when he described the last one, and Tom suspected he'd edited something. If it weren't so frightening and clearly harmful, it would be amusing to think of Seven of Nine, late of the Borg Collective, as a playful kitten or a wise old sculptor.

Paris was surprised by how upset he was. Distant, haughty, brilliant, and undeniably a knockout, Seven of Nine wasn't exactly what one would call endearing. But he had grown fond of her, and seeing her so helpless, so still, was alarming—and painful.

He didn't say anything, nor did the Doctor, as they moved among the injured. They mended broken bones, healed lacerations, offered a smile of encouragement. Well, Paris did, anyway. Finally they were done, but Tom made no move to leave.

"What? Aren't you going to bolt back for the bridge, free at last?"

Tom shook his head. Generally he enjoyed verbally sparring with the Doctor, but his concern was all for the unconscious woman on the diagnostic bed. "How's she doing?"

"Not well at all," said the Doctor, his voice laced with concern. "She's been unconscious for four hours. There's a great deal of brain activity and she has demonstrated rapid eye movement almost constantly." Now that he was standing by the bed, Tom could see that the Doctor spoke truly. Beneath their closed lids, Seven's eyes were darting about. It was the only movement about her still body—that and the barely perceptible rise and fall of her chest that told them she was still breathing.

"What's wrong with her?" Paris asked softly, more to himself than to the Doctor.

"I wish I knew. Too bad we can't see her birds. By my calculations, there are eight of them flapping around invisibly in my sickbay. Perhaps they could tell us something."

Seven could hear them talking. Their voices were distant, muffled, but she could catch words now and then. They penetrated her hallucinations, this living of other lives, like a gentle fragrance wafting toward her nostrils. But the voices went away again almost immediately. There was no place for them, no time. One doesn't concentrate on the smell of roses or the softness of their petals when one is about to die.

The skorrak bird had eluded her. Seven felt anger and frustration swell inside her and emitted a low growl. Her tail twitched.

"You stalked well, my little sweet Keela," her mother reassured her. The words were a comfort but the voice was vague and distracted. Seven glanced back and saw her mother staring up at the sky. She had been distantly aware of the cloud that had fallen over them, but now realized that it was no cloud at all. It was a ship, huge, square, floating in front of the life-giving sun and blocking its rays.

Seven knew fear. She had never seen anything like this vessel before. None of the people with whom they traded had that kind of ship. Who were they? What did they want? She padded back to her mother's side, the skorrak bird and her failure to catch it forgotten.

"Keela." Her mother's voice was calm. "Go inside. Now. Put through a message to the Council. Tell them—"

A blast of light burst from the ships. It reached clear to the ground and began to slice up chunks of Seven's world. The ground trembled and Seven fell hard. She splayed out her legs and dug her claws in an attempt to hold on as the earth bucked beneath her.

Buildings collapsed about her. Mammoth trees, centuries old, toppled and fell. How long this went on, Seven didn't know, but when she finally lifted her head she saw devastation beyond her ability to fully comprehend.

These intruders had not only shattered her world, they had taken it. From this vantage point, Seven could look down into the heart of the city. Except that the city was now completely gone. It had been scooped out like a cub might scoop a pawful of sand, and all that remained of a city that housed ten thousand souls was a huge, gaping tear in the good earth.

They came out of the shadowy jungle like walking nightmares. Bipedal, like the Graa, but unlike them in all other ways. Part pale flesh with no muzzles or fur, part black and frightening-looking machine, they charged forward, utterly unafraid. Seven yelped in terror. Her mother recovered and launched herself at the intruders, teeth and claws bare.

"Run, Keela! RUN!"

Seven froze, unable to obey. The intruders fired a strange weapon at her mother and the mighty huntress dropped like a stone. The intruder who slew her mother now lifted its eyes and fastened them on Seven. A single blue eye—the second had been replaced with a red light—stared at the small, cowering kitten. She— for it was female—parted full, gray lips and uttered a sentence:

"We are the Borg. Your biological and technological distinctiveness will be added to our own. Resistance is futile."

Without warning, Seven erupted into motion. She jerked in a series of violent convulsions, arching her chest up and slamming her head down hard. Paris and the Doctor leaped into action.

Tom fumbled for the right hypospray, his heart in his mouth. His fingers betrayed him and the instrument toppled off the tray to the floor. Before he retrieved it, cursing his clumsiness, Seven's flailing had ceased.

Cardiac arrest.

Seven of Nine was dying.

CHAPTER

9

DARKNESS. SILENCE. AND OUT OF THE SILENCE, A VOICE . . .

"Mother." A gentle shake. "Mother, wake up!"

"Kalti Druana? Honored Kalti, please . . ."

Seven shook off her sleep and sat up in her bed. Old bones and ancient muscles protested, but she ignored them. She had lived with the aches and pains of old age long enough so that they had become friends to the great artist. They were proof positive that she was still alive, that she had made it successfully through another day and had not slipped into the eternal darkness and silence that eventually waited to embrace her.

The children, her daughter Oplik and her daughter's mate Rel, had woken her. "What is it?" Seven asked sleepily. "What is wrong?"

"We are under attack," Rel replied somberly. "Orders have been given to the populace to congregate at certain areas. From there, they will try to transport us to more easily defensible ground."

Seven permitted herself a humorless smile. If her planet full of peaceful artists were indeed under attack, there was no place that was "defensible." They might run, frightened, but in the end, if a conqueror wished to take the planet, taken it would be. For millennia the Lennli had been undisturbed save for trading vessels. The planet held no strategic position, brought forth no unique minerals. Its treasure was its people and their talents, nothing more but certainly nothing less.

But she had to keep pretending, for the sake of the children. They stared at her with frightened eyes, pleading for her to say something that would somehow make everything all right.

She reached to stroke her daughter's cheek with a bright-red, seven-fingered hand. "Let us go," was all Seven could find to say.

The world she had known was no more. The thriving urban center near her home in the hills was under attack, and even as the three of them watched, the entire city was dug up with the conqueror's weapons and rose high in the air above them, floating with an incongruous grace toward the gaping maw of the waiting alien vessel.

They hadn't even made it to the transport vessel when the attack came. Dozens, perhaps hundreds of *the enemy came out of the night to descend on the fleeing populace. Rel, no warrior born, nonetheless fought to the death, taking one of the black-bodied, white-headed machine-beings with him. Oplik shrieked in horror at the sight of her mate's broken, bloody body lying on the purple grass. She was easy prey, gathered up into the arms of one of the obscenely evil intruders as if she weighed nothing at all.*

Through it all, Seven remained oddly calm. She grieved, bitterly and with all her sculptor's sensitive soul, for her people, for her children, but for herself, she could find little to lament. She had had a full life, with a loving mate and children who were a daily joy. She had sculpted all her life, and the only thing that caused her a moment's pain was the knowledge that her hands would never again caress simmik *stone.*

The one who claimed her was female, although only just. Young, still. And monstrous. As the woman-machine advanced purposefully on her, Druana demanded, "Who are you?"

"We are Borg." Arrogant, the voice and the eyes.

"No!" demanded Druana, turning the tables if only for a few seconds. "Who are you? What is your name?"

The abomination slowed, halted. "We are Borg," she repeated. "My designation is irrelevant." The Borg woman's eye—she had only one, bright blue and full of contempt—narrowed. She reached out for Druana and—

* * *

"She can't take much more of this."

"You've got to stop it. You said the part of the brain that was overstimulated was the, what, the—"

"Hippocampus, among other areas. Lieutenant, don't you think if I could stop this I would?"

Someone could. Dimly, Seven knew it. The image of nine black birds flying in a circle plucked at her mind. Someone could stop this. *When the pie was opened, the birds began to sing—*

They had her strapped down, the harsh metal casing crumpling her beautiful feathers. She wasn't supposed to be awake, Seven knew that much, but she was, though her voice died in her throat. She couldn't move her head, but her eyes darted about wildly. In the . . . pod? . . . beside her, she caught a glimpse of her beloved. Fresh terror flooded her. His left arm was gone, replaced by a black metal substitute. He had only one eye; the other socket was crammed with a twisted piece of machinery out of which a red light gleamed.

Sulmi!

Her heart ached for him, but he was no longer Sulmi, really, was he? He had become—what did the Destroyers call themselves—become Borg. She had heard the whispered tales, knew what the machine-things did to those they captured, or, as they coldly referred to it, "assimilated." It had been done to Sulmi, and now, it was being done to her, Amari, First of Six in her household.

She felt a sharp prick of pain as something was jabbed into her arm. Then, as she watched, one of the

Borg—a female—stepped forward and cut off her arm.

"Seven? It's Neelix. They tell me you've been having a pretty rough time of it." A pause. The sound of fidgeting. An image: a short, rather stout being with puffs of whiskers and a friendly countenance. Talaxian; Species 218. A man whose duties on the ship were many and varied.

"I thought I'd just pop in and tell you to hang on. Nobody knows what's going on inside that pretty head of yours but let me tell you, we miss you. We do! Why, did you know that you are the only one on the ship who actually likes my roast jak'ra? I promise I'll make you a special batch if—when you pull out of this."

A touch on her hand—warm, strong. "You're one of the toughest people I've ever met. You've got to pull through this, Seven." The voice grew husky. "You brought me back, you darn well better come back yourself. Please."

Seven chuckled to herself as her two little ones chased each other around her ankles. They had not yet mastered telepathy, so the warm spring air was filled with their happy chirps and trills. She glanced up at the sky, as she had done every day since word came that the Borg were heading toward their verdant planet. But her mate was the elected One of the continent of Ioh and the selected leader of the entire Circle of Seven, and he had reassured her that reinforcements would soon be arriving.

Still. The atrocities the Borg committed on those unfortunate enough to be assimilated were well known, and the thought of the monsters approaching their planet made Seven shiver. But surely the Emperor would honor the pact, would send his mighty battleships to protect the planet. Surely, there was a reason for the delay. Besides, the attack was not due for another six—

"What's that?" asked her youngest. Seven craned her long neck and followed his gaze.

Large cubical shapes were penetrating the atmosphere. And there was a voice—or rather hundreds, millions of voices—shattering the silence of the spring morning:

"We are the Borg. Prepare to be assimilated. Your biological and technological distinctiveness will be added to our own. Resistance is futile."

Tamaak! thought Rhiv. Tamaak, they are early!

Seven of Nine, lying prone on the diagnostic bed safely in sickbay, began to scream. She kept her eyes closed and opened her mouth in a large *O* and screamed from her very gut. She kept screaming, as Rhiv of Skeda was assimilated and her children placed in stasis tanks. As To-Do-Ka and Zarmuk and Shrri underwent the same ordeal. As one after the other of innocents were ripped from their lives and transformed into Borg. She felt the deaths of their personalities, sometimes the deaths of their physical bodies as well. They marched on in a merciless line, hundreds—no, thousands—of them. Their faces, their histories, their loves and losses and dreams were inextricably part of her and her body and mind writhed in agony as she died again and again.

Through the pain she heard voices, felt the warm press of hands, even of lips on her sweat-slicked forehead. She was told that she, Seven of Nine, was cared about, was safe, had value.

She didn't even recognize the name.

She was no one, and everyone. Designations meant nothing, and everything. She screamed until her voice was gone and even after that silent, heaving gasps erupted from her belly.

What are you doing?

The thought was launched at Imraak like an assault and the other Skedan reeled backward from the power of it. He stumbled, and caught himself.

What you ought to have done the moment we came aboard, he sent, his own thoughts hot and angry. *We have directed all our efforts toward this thing, this one, healing thing, and she stood in our way! She could have ruined everything!*

The other Skedans, alerted by the telepathic equivalent of shouting, had come forward and were staring at their leaders. Shemaak, her ears twitching in agitation, made as if to interrupt but Imraak raised a hand and impaled her with a furious glare. She halted, confused.

You are killing her! protested Tamaak.

Good.

She is an innocent! We do not kill—

Imraak's answer ripped through Tamaak's mind

and his head hurt violently. Gasping softly, he applied pressure behind his large ears as Imraak continued to rant.

An innocent? She is a Borg, Tamaak! Have you forgotten? Can it be that the loss of your mate and children means so little to you that you grieve for the injuring of the very one who took them?

Fury rose in Tamaak and he didn't bother to censor his thoughts. Imraak winced and those standing within two meters shrank back as well. *Do not wave the deaths of my family beneath my nose! You cannot possibly—*

He paused. Tamaak had been about to state that Imraak couldn't possibly know how he felt, but in truth, the other Skedan did. He, too, had lost family, though he had not yet taken a mate. Imraak's parents, siblings, his entire line, had been murdered when the Borg destroyed their capital city.

We agreed to distract her, so that she would not sense our weapon. And because of her crimes against our people and others, we agreed that we would torment her, rather than send her pleasant thoughts as we are doing for the rest of the crew. Nothing was said about this!

And will you stop it, elected One of the now-dead Ioh and alleged leader of the Circle of Seven? The contempt in Imraak's thoughts brought a sour smell to the room. *Will you grow soft, and pamper the poor little Borg like a pouchling? What is lost by having her memory destroyed? That might even be a kindness, considering what she has just undergone, might it not? If you stop this, you will put us all in jeopardy. If she is allowed a moment to think, to recall what she knows of us, she will find us out and then nothing we will have tried to do will bear fruit. Nothing!*

Tamaak's heart sank. Imraak, fueled by his hatred and cruelty, was nonetheless right. Seven of Nine was a threat to them, a threat they had successfully—if brutally—negated. He glanced around at his people, people who for the last several turns had trusted him implicitly. Could he turn on them now, for the sake of a Borg female they barely knew? The distraction they had planned had gotten out of hand. Imraak had overstepped the agreed-upon limits and pushed for his own, personal revenge. That could not be tolerated—but rectifying Imraak's transgression would put them all at risk. And that was unthinkable.

Tamaak swallowed his outrage. *We leave her as she is. But no more! If she recalls nothing, she cannot harm us. Let her be, Imraak.*

Imraak cocked his head and half-closed his eyes. His thoughts were shielded, but Tamaak didn't need to use his telepathic skills to know what his rival— for, by this action, so Imraak had declared himself to be—was thinking.

Imraak had won this round. He was planning on winning the next one.

At that moment, the door hissed open and Captain Janeway stalked in. Every line of her body indicated frustration and anger, and her eyes searched the group until they lit upon Tamaak. He hoped he did not appear unduly agitated to her eyes.

"Tamaak," she said stiffly, "I want a word with you."

* * *

By the time she had finished pouring the coffee—
Tamaak had said he was intrigued by the scent and
curious to taste it—Janeway had calmed down a
little. Her initial desire to confront him in front of
his people had faded immediately upon seeing him,
and in the end she'd decided to keep the meeting
private. They had retired to her ready room and now
gazed at one another over steaming cups of hot black
liquid.

"Captain, I am confused. Have we inadvertently
transgressed in some manner?" Tamaak asked, cock-
ing his head and looking troubled.

Janeway took a deep breath, let it out, and sipped
the coffee before replying. "I don't know. I hope not.
I'm sure you couldn't help but notice the ship's
rocking a few minutes ago."

Tamaak brought the cup to his muzzle and took a
tentative sip. His eyes half-closed. "Bitter, but bracing, and with a delicious, almost sweet undertone. I
like this coffee, Captain. Thank you for sharing it with
me. Yes, we noticed the activity. Is everything all
right?"

Janeway found herself wanting to tell Tamaak
more about the coffee rather than press for answers.
She gently directed her thoughts back to the matter
at hand. "We were attacked by an insectoid race.
They demanded that we turn you over to them.
Stationmaster Vooria couldn't get out of here fast
enough."

She held his gaze. "Tamaak, you must be honest

with me. What's going on? Why did Kraa want you so badly?"

At the mention of the insectoid race, Tamaak had spilled his coffee. He set the cup back in the saucer with a hand that trembled, and put it on the table.

"I had hoped we had shaken them," he said in a low voice. "The Ku travel with one companion, Captain Janeway, and that companion is death."

CHAPTER 10

"WHY DO THEY WANT YOU, TAMAAK? HAVE YOU DONE anything?"

He laughed—a short, harsh bark. "Captain, we are thirty-four refugees with no weapons. What could we possibly have done to anyone, let alone beings traveling in a ship? No, they want us, that is certain. But not because we have done anything. They want us for something they think we might do."

"What?"

He was silent, one of his fingers toying with the rim of the cup. "I have a confession, Captain." He lifted his gaze from the cup and pierced her with the anguish in the depths of his soft brown eyes. "We have not been completely honest with you. We knew this might happen. But it seemed so unlikely, the odds so great—perhaps you have wondered why we are refugees?"

"The thought had crossed my mind," Janeway admitted. "I didn't wish to pry."

"And I thank you for your discretion. Even though it happened years ago, it is still a painful subject among my people. We were struck down by a dreadful illness. It decimated the population. Millions died. The Skedans that you have in this vessel are all the Skedans in the universe, Captain Janeway."

"Oh, Tamaak," she breathed, the forgotten coffee growing cold in her cup. "I'm so sorry."

"We never found a cure for it—the Scarlet Death, we called it, because it inflamed all the visible membranes—but some of us survived it. It—it claimed the lives of my mate and two children."

Janeway said nothing, merely gazed with deep sympathy upon her friend. She let him continue in his own time.

"We had traded with many races, and the illness never jumped species. As far as we know, only Skedans caught the Scarlet Death, and only Skedans died from it. But fear is a dreadful thing, Captain. It can be as deadly as any disease. First, the other races stopped trading with us. We later discovered there was a quarantine placed upon our planet. We suffered badly from the lack of trade and more died who should not have."

His soft eyes flashed anger, which was almost immediately quelled as he composed himself. "When it was clear we had survived, we tried to relocate to another world. We were attacked, almost killed, by the very creatures who attacked you today. They are called the Ku, Captain Janeway. No doubt they have a name for themselves, but no warm-blooded creature knows it. They despise mammalian life-forms and hire themselves out as assassins to other non-mammalian races. They are extremely efficient. Tales of them haunt children's nightmares throughout this part of the galaxy. 'Behave, or the Ku will find you' is a common warning. Except among my people. We have been far too close to the Ku to tease our children with that kind of terror."

"Let me see if I understand you," said Janeway, putting her own cold cup of coffee on the table and leaning forward. "Skeda was decimated by a plague. Only a handful of people survived it. And instead of helping you, the other races of the Lhiaarian Empire shunned you and some even hired assassins to track your people down?"

He nodded sadly. "They fear that we are carriers of this disease. But they are in no danger. No one other than a native of Skeda has ever become ill."

"Tamaak, I'm so sorry. You have my word on it that I won't let these Ku take you."

"I thank you, Captain, and I deeply regret that your act of kindness toward my people has put your crew and ship in jeopardy."

"I must ask a favor, though."

"Name it."

"I'm going to require your people to be examined by our doctor. We'll need to see if there's any trace of a communicable disease and if we find it, we'll immediately get to work on producing a cure. Is that acceptable?"

He hesitated. "My people are very private, and we have faced judgment by other races before," he said. "Being forced to undergo an examination by an alien doctor will not sit well with them."

"I understand your emotions and I can't blame you for them, not after what you've undergone," said Janeway. "But surely you must see that we have to be certain. Tamaak," and she leaned forward and placed a gentle hand on his small, furred one, "we want to help you. We're your friends. We won't turn you over to the Ku and we'll help you to get to the Emperor, I promise. But you have to let us know that you don't pose a threat—even an unintentional one."

Finally, he nodded. "I will tell my people," he said as he rose. "Thank you for the coffee, Captain Janeway—and for your kindness. We do not carry this illness, but if you must see for yourselves, so be it."

As he stood alone in the turbolift, Tamaak Vriis berated himself. Careless! He had let himself get too caught up in his fondness for this new race, had not monitored Janeway's thoughts closely enough. He should not have let her take that next logical step of insisting that the Skedans be examined. He had been too busy gently guiding her to swallow the lie, and wrestling with his own guilt and anger at having to create that lie.

There had been some truth in it, enough truth to

make the whole lie palatable. But a lie it had been, and Tamaak found himself increasingly bothered about piling these falsehoods atop one another.

He wished he could trust this woman to stand by his people, to see the ultimate justice in their cause if she knew the whole story. But he dared not risk it. Too much was at stake. He could not destroy the hopes of his entire race because of sympathy toward strangers. The Borg woman must suffer, the captain must be lied to in the name of justice. He owed it to all the millions who had died, and the handful who still, despite everything, had survived.

No doubt Imraak would not approve and would suggest some countermeasure, such as wiping Captain Janeway's brain of the suggestion. Tamaak's jaw set in stubborn determination. That, he would not permit. True, erasing a thought would cause no permanent damage. But he had tampered enough with the minds of these innocent people. It was a matter of principle. Besides, this examination might not be as bad as he feared. Their doctor was as human as the rest of them; they could make sure that he saw only what they wished him to see. The secret would remain safe.

What was worse news was the revelation that the Ku had been sent after them. Tamaak had seen many horrors in his years, but the mere thought of the Ku, with their gleaming, chitinous bodies and multifaceted eyes filled with hatred, made even him shudder. There must have been a spy at the waystation where they had boarded *Voyager*. Now the most-feared killers in the galaxy knew where and how to find them. He silently thanked She-Who-Makes yet again for sending the Federation ship their way. Without the protection the vessel afforded, the Skedans would be extinct by now, for the Ku wouldn't even spare little Thena. They slew not just for money, but for pleasure.

But even *Voyager* would have a difficult time defending itself against the Ku's technology. Already quite advanced themselves, the hired assassins had received technology from every culture with which they dealt. The result was small, fast ships with incredible attack and defense systems that were piloted by creatures with one thing on their minds: *Kill the Warms.*

He shook his head and concentrated. Fear would do nothing. He had to cooperate with the *Voyager* crew as much as possible without jeopardizing his mission. All of their lives—Skedan and human—depended on it.

"Lieutenant Torres," said Vorik in his mild voice, "if I may say so, cursing will not make the repairs go faster nor increase their efficacy."

Torres lay on her back beneath the console. The warp drive had picked this time to begin whining for attention. Captain Janeway was insisting at warp eight, warp nine if possible, and the vessel was protesting at the constant demand. It had been a while since they'd done maintenance work and *Voyager* was not going to let them forget it.

She had muttered under her breath, cursed aloud, yelled, and once even banged a tool furiously against the casing. Vorik was right. Such displays of temper would not make the repairs go faster nor increase their efficacy.

But they made her feel a little better.

She took a deep breath, held it, and counted to ten before sliding back out.

"Sorry," she growled.

"An apology is not necessary. I was merely—"

"Well, merely don't, okay?" Her voice rose and to her horror the last word caught on an unexpected and certainly unwelcome lump in her throat.

Tom. What's wrong? What have I done?

Vorik cocked his head and scrutinized her. She glared back, blinking rapidly. Damn it, she was not about to break down in front of this Vulcan who—

"You have been working steadily for three hours, twenty-seven minutes, and nine seconds," the Vulcan observed. "May I respectfully request that we take a break? I would like to buy you a cup of raktajino."

"Vorik, I thought we—"

"And listen. I perceive that there is something on your mind."

Torres softened a little. "That's awfully kind of you, Vorik, but—"

"Kindness is only a portion of it," continued Vorik. "Your hostility and frustration is affecting your performance as head of Engineering."

That made her smile a little. Trust a Vulcan to be practical above all else. Her neck and shoulders were beginning to ache from the strain of working in such cramped quarters. Maybe it *was* time for a cup of icy raktajino.

"You're on."

As she sipped the cold, strong beverage in the mess hall, she listened to Vorik make small talk. Vulcan small talk was something entirely different from the human variety. It was chock-full of information and delivered in a cool, clipped manner. Yet nothing that Vorik imparted was of any real consequence, factual though it was, and she found that the steady drone of an unemotional voice was quite soothing. He was more perceptive than he let on.

She was aware that Vorik knew that whatever it was that was going on between her and Tom was not going on right now. With a slightly sick feeling in her stomach that had nothing at all to do with the strong dose of caffeine it had just received, Torres acknowledged that probably *everybody* knew. It was a small ship, as she had told Tom before.

But she just couldn't figure it out. Ever since the Skedans had come on board, Tom had been ignoring her in favor of "showing our guests around." One guest in particular, a cute little big-eyed female, seemed to command a great deal of his attention. She growled into her raktajino. Lieutenant Tom Paris certainly had a reputation as a ladies' man before they had begun—seeing each other? Dating? B'Elanna couldn't even come up with an appropriate term—but she'd never thought he'd turn into some intergalactic cradle-robber, dropping her for a teenaged talking kangaroo, cute and big-eyed as it might be.

In the end, she made small talk herself. She wasn't about to share her worries with Vorik or anyone else. She would keep them close like something rare and precious, as she had kept secrets and fears all her life; in her heart for her and her alone to see, to take out and examine on the long nights when she couldn't sleep.

The bracing beverage and the twenty minutes or so of shop talk helped. By the time Torres and Vorik rose to return to Engineering, Torres had made her decision.

To hell with Tom Paris. She loved him, yes, and he knew it. If that wasn't enough for him, if he was willing to let whatever they had—and damn it, it was good—slip between his fingers, then that was his decision. She'd faced her demons by telling him. She had peace, of a sort, in her heart. B'Elanna Torres, half-human, half-Klingon, fully welcome in neither world, was used to loneliness.

She'd just have to get used to it again.

The woman on the diagnostic bed opened her eyes. Her body ached with weariness and her head throbbed. Even breathing was laborious.

She could identify nothing. There was a familiarity about this place, but no words, no names came to mind. The metal arching over her body—she knew it; the being puttering about with a tray full of tools was someone she recognized.

As she opened her mouth to speak, there was a brief flash of pleasure: *I know how to communicate.*

"Hello?" Her voice was raspy, her lips dry. The person over at the little table spun around, his eyes wide.

"Seven?"

She frowned a little. "Seven what?" There were birds, of course, but there were ten of them, not seven, and they were quiet. She ignored them, more curious about this place and this man.

The man did not reply. He took one of the tools and passed it over her head. "Oh, no," he said softly, and when his eyes met hers they were full of compassion.

"Seven . . . do you remember who I am? What this place is?"

She shook her head, sitting up when the man pressed a button and the curving arc of metal retreated back into the bed. She swung her long legs down and reached to touch her face.

"I don't know anything—yet I think I should. Why do you keep repeating that number? What is my name?" Suddenly afraid, she drew her legs up toward her chest and clasped her hands around them tightly.

"Please don't be frightened. It's going to be all right. Somehow. You may call me the Doctor. You are—"

Memories. Flashes of light, of images, of fear and wonderful smells and green and metal and embraces, soft fabric against her skin, fear that shook her to the bone.

She reached again to touch her face. Something cold and metallic was on it, and she fingered it gently. Her brow furrowed. She reached up and unclasped her hair, combing it out with her fingers.

"Doctor," she said softly, "I remember. I know who I am."

* * *

"And that's the situation," finished Janeway. She had been watching her senior staff carefully as she briefed them on what her conversation with Tamaak Vriis had yielded. A warm glow of pride flickered in her breast. They were all in danger as long as the Skedans remained on their ship. The logical thing to do would be to go ahead and surrender them to these Ku and avoid another fight.

But, Tuvok and Vorik aside, this crew had never been about logic. They'd always been about heart, about compassion, and there had never been a better opportunity to demonstrate it than now. Janeway had never seen a better example of innocence wronged than in the Skedans. Provided that Tamaak's theory about the Scarlet Death's inability to jump species proved correct, she could present her findings to the Emperor and ask for clemency on behalf of a race that had already had to bear more hardships than anyone ought to. And with the Skedan's amazing diplomatic touch, she might be able to get that safe passage for her own crew as well.

Her senior staff clearly shared her sentiments. There was not one comment, not a "however," not even from Tuvok. Janeway of course had the authority to go forward with her decision regardless of what her staff thought, but it was always easier when everyone was of one mind—and one heart.

"I'm not overly fond of bugs anyway," said Tom, his comment bringing forth smiles and nods.

"Then we proceed. We travel at yellow alert—the Ku might find us at any time. We—"

"Sickbay to Janeway."

"Janeway here. What is it, Doctor?"

"You'd better get down to sickbay right away."

He refused to elaborate. Janeway left the bridge in Chakotay's capable hands and hastened to sickbay. Her imagination took all kinds of twists and turns. What in God's name had happened to poor Seven now?

The door hissed open and Janeway got her first shock. Seven looked fine, though a little tired. She was sitting up, her legs dangling off the side of the bed—swinging, more accurately—and was busily devouring a plate of something Neelix had brought her. The little Talaxian stood at her side, beaming.

"Captain," said the Doctor in a voice she couldn't interpret, "I would like to introduce you to Annika Hansen."

CHAPTER

11

JANEWAY COULD ONLY STARE. SEVEN OF NINE LOOKED UP from the food she was eating with her fingers—something brown; Janeway was willing to bet it was chocolate—and wiped sheepishly at the crumbs on her lips.

"Hi," she said shyly.

The words broke the captain's shocked paralysis and she tentatively stepped toward the diagnostic bed. "Sev—Annika? How are you feeling?"

"I was kind of tired, but Neelix brought me some chocolate cake, and believe me I was going to sit up for *that*. I had some on my last birthday and it's delicious!" She turned the full radiant force of a genuine smile on the Talaxian and he blushed a little.

Good God, thought Janeway. *She's beautiful!*

There had never been any doubt in anyone's mind that Seven of Nine, late of the Borg, was an attractive woman. A strong, fit figure coupled with a beautiful face ensured that perception. But she had always been, to Janeway's mind, like Pygmalion's statue—cold, without the spark of warmth to make her fully human, fully alive. Her beauty wasn't truly realized.

Seven of Nine was no Vulcan. She had emotions, but they tended toward the darker side of the spectrum. Janeway had seen her angry, hate-filled, and frightened. She'd never seen her smile like this, openly and honestly, a smile that crinkled her eyes and lit up her face.

Tears started in her eyes unexpectedly and the captain blinked them back. Here was the woman she had hoped to see blossom on *Voyager,* one who was truly human despite the alien implants that remained in her body. Seven of Nine's brain had still functioned like a Borg's. But now, it was almost like a miracle. She had been reborn.

"Annika," Janeway breathed, reaching out a hand to stroke the soft flesh of Seven's cheek. "Annika Hansen. Welcome back."

At the senior staff meeting Janeway called immediately after meeting their newest crew member, the Doctor held everyone's attention. On the viewscreen was a diagram of Seven of Nine's brain, complete with implants, to which he gestured frequently.

"As the old cliché goes, hindsight is twenty-twenty. When Seven of Nine—Annika—was suffering her hallucinations, I regret to admit that I had no idea what they were. I believe now, judging from subsequent events, that they were memories."

"Memories?" scoffed Paris. He was seated as far away from a clearly unhappy Torres as it was possible to be and yet still be present for the meeting. "To the best of my knowledge, Seven of Nine was never a kitten." He paused, thought about it, and opened his mouth as if to comment further. The Doctor quickly interrupted him.

"That is correct. She was also never violated by Kovan," he reminded them. He was alluding to a memory that had returned to Seven, or what had at least seemed a memory. She had been convinced that Kovan, an arms merchant with whom they had been negotiating, had attacked her and forcibly extracted dormant Borg nanoprobes. A subsequent investigation had proved the man innocent—the memory of a violation, while probably genuine at its origin, had been distorted—but not before Kovan had taken his own life.

"The incident with Kovan is a cautionary tale for me," the Doctor confessed. "Given Seven of Nine's extremely traumatic history, heaven knows what's stirring in that brain of hers. I was reluctant to jump to any sort of conclusion without solid proof."

"But . . . why does she remember being someone else?" asked Harry.

"As a Borg, Seven of Nine assimilated hundreds of races. The Graa, the felinoid race, was definitely among them. She told us as much. I'm willing to bet that the others were too. And when the Borg assimilate a race—"

"They take the essence of who they are," finished Chakotay. "Everything they know, the Collective has access to."

"Precisely," approved the Doctor. "So these hallucinations are indeed memories, but not Seven of Nine's. The onslaught of memories was too much for her and her brain shut down, blocking *all* memories in an attempt to prevent becoming overstimulated. For a brief while, Seven of Nine was a blank slate. She is beginning to recover her memories, starting with those from her childhood."

"Which is why she insists on being called Annika," said Harry. "The name—the designation—Seven of Nine means nothing to her. She *is* Annika Hansen."

"She isn't behaving like a child," said Janeway.

"No. Her memories are not gone, they are simply being blocked. Essentially, she has amnesia. She remembers how to walk, speak, eat—basic things. But the details of her life, who she was and is, are eluding her."

"What about the birds?" asked Chakotay. "Is she still seeing them?"

The Doctor frowned. "Yes, and I still believe they are significant in some way."

"Will she recover her memories fully?" asked Torres. "She's not going to be a lot of help to us if all she can remember are birthday parties and nursery rhymes."

"I see no reason to believe she won't," the Doctor replied. "There seems to be no permanent damage. The human brain is a complex and marvelous thing. Even now, we still don't fully understand it. But we have recorded everything since she came on board. I'll let her become familiar with the logs and if any of you would like to come and talk with her, remind her of incidents that have occurred, that will probably help stimulate her memories as well. I am *not,* however, going to engage her in psychoanalysis this time. What I will do is attempt to artificially manipulate various memory centers in her brain. In the meantime, I suggest you enjoy Annika. She's much simpler than Seven of Nine."

"Restoring Seven's memory is a top priority, Doctor," said Janeway. "However, I've got something else you need to do as well. You'll need to run a complete medical analysis on all the Skedans, from Tamaak down to the littlest pouchling. We've got to make sure they're not carrying the Scarlet Death."

"Good heavens. What a workload. Where would you be if you had only a simple human doctor?"

Tamaak, as leader of his people—as far as everyone but the hostile Imraak was concerned—volunteered to be the first to undergo the examination. He would be able to tell the rest of them how best to approach the doctor's mind.

When he entered sickbay, the doctor glanced up from a padd. "Ah. And which one are you?"

"Greetings, Doctor . . . ?"

The doctor sighed heavily. "Just Doctor will do."

"Then I am just Tamaak." He half-closed his eyes in a smile and tentatively reached out to touch the Doctor's mind.

Nothing.

He inhaled swiftly, shocked. The Doctor wasn't flesh—he didn't have a mind to manipulate!

"Something wrong?"

"Of course not. I am only a little nervous." What was he? A machine? He hazarded a guess. "I am told," he lied, "that you are an artificial intelligence of some sort. I am curious. Please tell me more."

"I am an Emergency Medical Hologram. I was activated shortly after *Voyager* entered the Delta Quadrant. Sit on the diagnostic bed, please," said the Doctor. Tamaak obliged. A hologram. Just his luck. This Doctor was brusque and clearly very efficient. He turned to select an instrument and in that brief instant Tamaak closed his eyes and calmed his mind.

Telepathy was a skill among his people. Just as all humans had the physical ability to run but some could run faster than others, all Skedans had the ability to use telepathy, but some were better at using it than others. It was a conscious choice, like speaking, and just like speaking it produced something that could be recorded by instruments. In fact, it already had, but up until now the Skedans could manipulate the crew's minds and regulate how much they saw.

But the Doctor had no brain to play with, and would immediately see the mental activity on his medical instruments. Tamaak briefly calmed himself and shut down all telepathic activity. It was not an easy thing to do, but most Skedans did it. Even among telepaths, there were times when one wanted privacy. One didn't have to broadcast one's thoughts all the time.

So he sat, attempting to be calm and composed, while this holographic doctor ran various instruments over him, drew samples, monitored heart rate, and in general poked, probed, and prodded.

"As you are a species that is unfamiliar to us, I don't have a baseline against which to compare your health. But from what I've been able to determine here, you appear to be fine, Tamaak. The real answers to any questions the captain might have about your people lie in here," and he gestured to an instrument he had used to gather samples. "I'll run every test I can think of on these and we should have the results in a few hours. I'll notify you and the captain if there's anything unusual. In the meantime, you're free to go. Please send in the next Skedan for examination."

He had done it. The Doctor had picked up no traces of unusual brain activity. Tamaak bowed his head on his long, thin neck and strolled out of sickbay. Once he entered the corridor, he hastened his stride.

This could spell disaster. Not everyone controlled his or her telepathic ability as masterfully as Tamaak Vriis, which was why he had been chosen to lead the Council of Seven. Certainly the little ones who could barely walk on their own couldn't be expected to exercise the subtle control that was required.

Tamaak said a quick prayer to She-Who-Creates to protect them. He hoped that it would be enough.

* * *

Annika knew that the black birds who kept her company—she counted quickly; the number had crept up to eleven—could be seen only by her. The Doctor had told her something about trauma and recovered memories and hallucinations and the activities of the subconscious in an attempt at self-preservation, but all she really knew was that everything, every person and tool and room and decoration, that she encountered was familiar and strange at the same time, and the birds were a welcome constant.

Chakotay was walking with her. He was taking her on an extended tour of a ship that she once, he assured her, knew like the back of her hand. Annika bowed her golden head and glanced at her hand, which was covered with strange metal and tubes. It was hardly something she knew well, as the phrase might have indicated.

"And this is the aeroponics bay," he said as the door hissed open. A rush of warm, humid air laden with a sweet scent hit her nostrils and she breathed deep.

"Oh, it's beautiful!" Annika gasped. She stepped forward and touched the silky petals of a red flower in full bloom. It felt exquisite against her fingers. "Don't tell me—this is my favorite place on the ship, right?"

Chakotay smiled a little. "Hardly. Your interest in the aeroponics bay is limited to how efficiently it produces nutritional supplements."

She wrinkled her nose. "Really?"

"You've been known to say that beauty is irrelevant."

She made a face and returned her attention to the

flower. "I'm afraid this Seven of Nine of yours sounds like she was a stick in the mud."

He laughed out loud at that. "I'm afraid you're right. But we were all fond of her—*are* fond of you. Come on. There's a lot more to see."

The birds had lit on some of the plants and as Annika turned to go, one of them started pecking at the red flower. "Hey!" she chastised, waving her arm at the bird. "Leave it alone. Come on."

Chakotay tensed. "Your birds?"

"Yes." Annika sighed. "I know you can't see them, but I sure can. The Doctor says it means something, but he doesn't know what."

Chakotay's lips curved in a smile. "I have a theory," he said, mysteriously.

"What? I'm dying to know what they mean!"

"Let's give your memory a little time to heal, shall we? You may come up with the answer yourself. In the meantime, the next stop is your old post—Astrometrics."

Kathryn Janeway stared at the stars rushing past on the viewscreen, but her thoughts were distant. They were on a Starfleet vessel that was long gone, called the *Raven*. On that ship the classic trinity of man, woman, and child had played out a tragic scenario.

Seven had already been through that particular trauma. The memory had come, threatened to destroy her and those who had befriended her, and finally been resolved.

Would she go through it again, this time—for the second time—as Annika Hansen? What would it do to her? Would she relive the violation of assimilation? Would she become Borg once those memories returned, or would there be anything of Annika, of the Seven who had become a crewmate?

Tough questions, and Janeway didn't even know what to hope for.

"Captain," said Paris, startling her out of her reverie, "we're closing in on Waystation Number 109."

She uncrossed her legs and sat up straight in her captain's chair. "Bring us out of warp, Lieutenant."

The vessel slowed to impulse power. Waystation Number 109 was a homely thing. No green signs of life on this planet. It was a barren rock, save where the evidence of technology marred its plain countenance. There were many ships in orbit about the Imperial checkpoint. Janeway had opted not to cancel yellow alert, although at this point no one appeared to offer them a hostile reception. They had been through too much for her to not be as cautious as possible at this juncture.

"Captain, we're being hailed," Kim said.

So far, so good, Janeway thought to herself. This was exactly how things had played out at the other waystation, until of course things had gone drastically bad.

"Onscreen," she ordered.

The visage of a new alien race appeared. In contrast to the Lhiaarians, this one was humanoid, the only exception being a split upper lip, no visible ears, and plating across the head. Catlike eyes gazed at the captain and slit nostrils flared. Janeway recognized the yellow-and-red official insignia of a stationmaster on the being's shoulder.

"Waystation 109 to approaching unknown vessel, please identify yourself," droned the alien stationmaster in a bored male voice.

Here goes nothing, thought Janeway. She lifted her chin.

"I'm Captain Kathryn Janeway of the Federation Starship *Voyager*. We are hoping to—"

That was as far as she got.

The screen went blank. From among the masses of ships, ten behemoths separated themselves out and flew straight toward *Voyager*. Immediately Janeway recognized them as Imperial transport vessels.

"Red alert!" she cried. "All hands, battle stations!"

No sooner had she gotten the words out than the ships veered off. Huge cargo bay doors that comprised most of the length of the Imperial ships slowly opened. And pouring forth, with all the purpose and implacability of locusts descending on Pharaoh's crops, were dozens of small, black, shiny Ku ships.

CHAPTER

12

CLEVER. THOUGHT JANEWAY, OUTRAGE AT THE DECEPTION welling inside her. *They hid in the bellies of the Imperial vessels so that we wouldn't realize they were here—just waiting for us.*

The shields were already up, but *Voyager* took a beating nonetheless as the round, evil-looking ships proceeded to fire upon them.

"Damage report!"

"Shields down eighteen percent, still holding," intoned Tuvok. "Seventeen casualties on decks seven, four, eight, and twelve."

"Return fire," she ordered. "Janeway to Chakotay,

report to bridge immediately." A pause, then, "Bring Annika with you. This ought to jolt her memory."

The black Ku ships fired again. Again the ship pitched under the attack, and this time several bridge members hurtled out of their seats. Someone cried out in pain. Casualty on the bridge.

"Shields down twenty-six percent. More casualties are coming in. Lieutenant Torres reports that the warp engine is off-line."

Tuvok uttered the devastating news in a calm voice. Janeway's gut clenched and her palms grew wet. The last time they had encountered the determined Ku, they had escaped by fleeing to a safer place. He who fights and runs away, et cetera. But this time that wasn't an option, and Janeway only now realized how much she had depended on that option.

They were sitting ducks.

She set her jaw and willed away the fear for her crew's safety. "Keep firing. Hammer them, Tuvok. Don't let up. We've got nothing to lose now. As for the Imperial vessels, don't fire at them unless fired upon. I'm still not sure how deeply they're involved in this."

"Aye, Captain."

The Vulcan security officer was as good as his word. *Voyager* became the attacker now, firing an almost steady stream of phasers. It looked as if Janeway's plan was working. The small black Ku ships ceased their own attack momentarily, darting away to avoid the Federation vessel's aggressive, almost brutal assault.

During the entire engagement, the Imperial ships

sat by, doing nothing. They had assisted the Ku by offering vessels in which the insectoid beings could hide, but now that an active battle had begun it was obvious that the representatives of the Lhiaarian Empire did not wish to be drawn into it.

These Ku, these assassins, as Tamaak had described them, clearly exerted a powerful influence. Fear had a long reach and a strong hand.

But Janeway wasn't afraid. She was angry.

Voyager scored another direct hit on a Ku vessel with little, if any, apparent damage. "What are those ships made of, anyway?"

She heard footsteps and glanced up to see Chakotay and Annika. She saw that Annika had exchanged Seven of Nine's severe hair and outfit for flowing blond locks and a loose, breezy red dress. Janeway's eyes flickered back to the viewscreen as Chakotay sat down beside her.

Another direct hit. Another strike with nothing to show for it.

"I don't get it," said Tom. "Nothing should be able to take a beating like that."

Behind her, Janeway heard a soft gasp. She turned to find Annika clutching the railing. The young woman's eyes were wide, her mouth open in a soundless cry. Her body was rigid, locked in paralysis.

"Annika?" No response. "Seven?"

Species 13. Insectoid, able to adjust the density of their exoskeleton to comply with various environments. Hostile and intelligent. Assimilation was diffi-

cult. Advanced technologically. Their distinctiveness added to the efficacy of Borg assimilation.

"Captain!" She breathed again, a great gasp of air. "Reconfigure the phasers to a random pattern."

Janeway didn't waste valuable time asking why. "Do it," she shouted to Tuvok.

The next phaser fire that contacted a Ku vessel shattered it. There was a brief flash of light in the starry sky and pieces of wreckage flew everywhere.

"Continue firing."

"Captain, the random configuration does enable us to fight back," replied Tuvok. "However, shields are down to sixteen percent. Another direct hit from them and they could be completely decimated."

"Captain," said Kim, "We're being hailed."

"Onscreen."

The by-now loathed visage of the hideous alien captain filled the screen. His antennae waving and mandibles clicking, Kraa T'Krr spoke.

"Captain Janeway, our information tells us you cannot take another direct hit. We offer you generous terms of surrender. Relinquish your passengers to us, and we will not harm you or your vessel."

"He is lying, Captain," snapped—who? Annika? Seven of Nine? Janeway didn't know anymore. "The Tuktak despise all warm-blooded beings. It is an integral part of their culture. They want the Skedans alive so that they can ritually dismember them as part of their assassination contract. As for us, we serve no purpose and they will destroy us once they have what they want."

Her back was straight, her eyes cold and angry as she gazed upon Kraa. Janeway had no reason to doubt her certainty. The captain returned her gaze to the screen, stared at the unfathomable creature before her, then said in clipped, measured tone, "Your proposal is unacceptable. You want the Skedans for ritual dismemberment and us for target practice? Not on my watch."

She jerked her head in Harry's direction and at once the screen went blank.

"Tuvok, fire at will. Tom, evasive maneuvers. We know how to hurt them now, let's stay out of range as long as we—"

Two more Ku vessels were blown apart by the random patterned phaser blasts. *Voyager* maneuvered with the grace and control that Janeway so loved, guided by the skilled input of a pilot to whom flying was almost as natural as breathing.

The powerful shots missed them. For a wild, joyful moment Janeway thought they could actually do it. Hell, there were only, what, sixty-odd ships. Now that Seven had revealed the Ku's weakness, *Voyager* was blasting them from the skies. All they had to do was keep firing and not get fired upon themselves.

The ship rocked violently. The conn spat fire and smoke and Tom Paris cried out and toppled from his seat. His face was blackened and he covered it with his arms, groaning. But there was no time for sympathy.

"Our shields are gone," said Tuvok.

Janeway swallowed, glanced over at Chakotay. His

dark eyes bored into hers and he nodded, once. One more solid blast would do it.

"Keep firing," she told her security officer, proud and surprised at how steady her voice was. "We're going to take as many of them with us as—"

Her voice caught in her throat despite her best intentions as she realized the cursed little black oval ships were powering up for a final attack. She leaped out of her chair and pounced on the conn, keying in a desperate, final twist and turn in an almost certainly futile effort to minimize the blast's effects on the helpless ship.

For what purpose? her mind screamed. *Why delay the inevitable for a few more seconds? What will it get you, Kathryn?*

"Captain!" Tuvok's voice registered surprise. "Forty vessels are approaching, heading six mark—"

"I see them," breathed his captain, her eyes glued to the screen in wonderment.

They were no polished fleet, these ships. They were a motley crew, all shapes, sizes, designs, colors, and speeds, but they moved with a uniform purpose to position themselves between the damaged Federation vessel and her would-be predators. They fired as they came, doing no damage but providing a blessed distraction as they drew Ku fire.

Voyager danced between the ships, firing and rolling. Janeway didn't quite have Tom's finesse at the controls but she knew her ship, knew what it could do. In the spaces between the mysterious but welcome ships, she piloted her vessel, fired, and ducked back to safety. Janeway's jaw was set so hard it ached, her fingers flying over the controls.

Another Ku ship destroyed, and she felt a quick flush of pleased excitement. Janeway didn't like the sensation. It was deeply ingrained in her to fight only when provoked, to disable the enemy, not destroy them. But she didn't know enough about the peculiar Ku vessels to target only the engines and weapons systems. She barely knew enough to even fight back. She had no reason to like the Ku, particularly if everything Tamaak and Annika/Seven had told her about them was true. But the deep thrill of animal pleasure that coursed through her veins as she blew them out of the sky disgusted her.

Another one down. And another. *Voyager* dove and darted, evading the single blast that would bring her down. Her unknown allies seemed not to know the secret of fighting the Ku, and kept blasting away ineffectively. But they were there, shielding Janeway and her crew, and she was grateful to the core of her being.

"Captain," said Chakotay, "It looks like they're falling back."

"We have destroyed seven of the enemy vessels," said Tuvok. "Commander Chakotay is correct. The Ku, or the Tuktak as Seven has dubbed them, are indeed retreating."

An instant later, Janeway's own eyes confirmed Tuvok's statement. The black ovals banded together, then, moving as one, they went into warp. The Imperial ships lingered for a few moments while Janeway held her breath. Would they attack now, too?

There was a long, tense moment in which no one—not the Imperial ships, not the mystery rescuers, and not the Starfleet ship—moved.

And then, lacking the grace of the Tuktak vessels, the Imperial transport ships turned away from the field of battle and headed back toward the waystation.

Janeway began to tremble as the adrenaline ebbed. She closed her eyes in relief for a second, then returned her attention to repairing the damage. She'd start with the wounded.

Sliding out of the chair, she knelt beside the limp body of Tom Paris. She pressed a finger to his pulse—erratic, but there. He looked like hell. His handsome face was burned, the flesh baked and cracked. She hoped there was no permanent damage.

"Emergency medical transport. Lock onto Paris's signal and beam him to sickbay *now.*"

She watched as Paris's body shimmered, then disappeared. She rose on legs that trembled and felt pain shoot through her knee. Obviously, at some point she'd torn the ligaments doing . . . something.

"Anybody else hurt?" The rest of the bridge team seemed to have survived intact. She limped toward her chair and sank into it.

"Captain," said Kim, "We're being hailed."

"I do *not* want to talk to another stationmaster right now, Harry. Tuvok, damage report."

"Captain," insisted Kim, "it's not from the waystation. It's from our friends."

A smile touched her lips. "Onscreen."

"It's audio only," Kim said, putting it through.

The voice that rang through the bridge had been mechanically distorted. It buzzed and hummed, but the words were understandable.

"Captain Janeway?"

"Yes, I'm Captain Kathryn Janeway of the Starship *Voyager*. Please identify yourself. I'd like to be able to thank the person who saved our lives by name."

"I regret that I cannot comply at this time, Captain," replied the artificial voice. "I have instructions for you, and you must obey them to the letter."

Janeway frowned. She glanced over at Chakotay and saw her own doubt and concern mirrored on his dark face.

"Whoever you may be, I am grateful to you for my life and those of my crew. But I don't take kindly to being instructed—"

"Captain. I must insist. You have seen what the Ku can do. You know what they want. If you wish to survive and keep the Skedans aboard alive as well, you must comply with my instructions."

She thought about her ship, damaged and unable to go to warp for who knew how long. Janeway took a deep breath.

"What are these instructions?"

"You must proceed directly to the Lhiaarian home-world, bearing four-six—"

"I know where it is," said Janeway. "Why?"

"You must follow the specific route we are transmitting to your operations officer. This is the only route on which we can guarantee your safety. Once you have reached Lhiaari," the mechanical voice continued, ignoring her pointed question, "You will have an audience with Emperor Beytek. You have friends on Lhiaari, Captain. You may count on this. But we can continue to protect you only if you obey these instructions."

Janeway was stunned. That quickly, that unexpectedly, she was assured of an audience with the Emperor—the very thing they had been seeking since they entered Lhiaarian Imperial space.

She thought for a moment. These people, while their identities were unknown, had certainly saved her skin. They seemed to know exactly what was going on. They knew the Ku, knew the Skedans were on board, and promised an audience with the single most difficult person to contact in the sector.

"Silence audio," she told Kim. "Annika, do you—does Seven—recognize these vessels?"

The young woman frowned and chewed her lower lip, concentrating. Finally, she shook her head.

"I don't know," she replied. "They don't appear to be familiar, but . . ." Her voice trailed off. Little was familiar to her now, and they all knew it.

Janeway nodded her comprehension. "Suggestions?" she asked, glancing from Chakotay to Tuvok.

"It could be a trap," said Tuvok. "We could possibly be getting ourselves entangled in a political struggle of some sort. These could be pirates, intervening to save us only to lure us away and attempt a capture of their own. It is difficult for me to recommend trusting anyone at this juncture, and their insistence that we follow a specific route is suspicious."

"That's possible," agreed Chakotay. "And I don't like the fact that they won't identify themselves. However, as the old saying goes, actions speak louder than words, and their actions fairly shout out loud. Besides, the Lhiaarian homeworld was our destination anyway. It seems we have a lot of enemies, and perhaps that one route is the only secure way for us to get to Lhiaari. I don't see the harm in continuing on and seeing how this scenario plays out. It couldn't be any worse than continuing blindly."

Janeway nodded. Her two most important advisors both had good points, but she tended to think as Chakotay did. "The only other option would be to head for unclaimed space, and there's no reason to believe that the Tuktak, or the Ku, or whoever the hell they are, won't follow us. We'll stay at yellow alert and continue on our course," she said. "It'll give us time to effect repairs and get the warp engine back on line, I hope. If there is trouble, I want to face it able to fight or flee, if necessary. Harry, put our mysterious ally back on."

"Captain? Time is fleeting."

"Let me make one thing clear, friend," said Janeway. "I don't trust people I don't know, and I don't know you. But I will follow your instructions—for the moment." She hesitated, added, "Again, we are grateful for your assistance. Janeway out."

She listened, absently rubbing her aching knee as Tuvok gave her the damage report. It was pretty bad. The Doctor would have his hands full, and so would Torres. A thought crossed her mind.

"Janeway to Torres."

"Torres here." The chief engineer sounded frazzled. "Captain, no offense, but I'm aware of the damage and I'm on it, so—"

"Lieutenant," said Janeway, keeping her voice mild, "Lieutenant Paris was injured pretty badly. He's in sickbay right now. The ship is out of immediate danger. I think Carey and Vorik and the rest of your team can spare you for ten minutes."

Silence. Then, quietly, "Thank you, Captain."

"Captain," said Annika/Seven. "Request permission to visit Engineering. I believe—I believe some of my memories are returning and I might be able to offer assistance."

Janeway gazed at her. Annika/Seven stood straighter, her eyes were cooler, her face more composed, than had been the case when Janeway last saw her in sickbay. The soft, loose red fabric of her dress, which suited her just a few moments ago, now seemed childish and inappropriate. There was still warmth in her voice, animation in her movements. Annika was still present. But for how much longer?

"The Tuktak defense systems," Janeway said, figuring it out as she spoke. "The ability to reconfigure their ship's shields—the Borg assimilated that technology, didn't they? Except Borg vessels were too large for such a field to be practical. Instead, they turned that technology toward establishing personal shields for the Borg drones."

"That is correct," said Annika/Seven. "The Tuktak are an ancient race. They were among the first few species we assimilated. Thanks to their shielding technology, the Borg have become nearly invincible."

Pride. Coolness. "We," the Borg.

Janeway felt a pang of unexpected loss as she gazed at the beautiful face. She had a feeling that Annika Hansen would not be around much longer.

CHAPTER
13

PRIANA LISTENED DISINTERESTEDLY AS TAMAAK FILLED them in on the final results of their examinations with the doctor. All of the Skedans, right down to the infants in the pouches, had been to sickbay.

Because he is a non-organic, I cannot read his thoughts, know precisely what he knows. But I can guess. Most of us were able to resist the urge to use our telepathic powers. For that, I commend you. I know how difficult it is. But some of us weren't, especially the younger ones. It is my hope that the Doctor will assume that this is a natural function of the younger members of our race. Just as our metabolisms are faster as we are younger, he may assume this is nothing more than something that disappears as we age. We can—Priana!

Priana jumped, startled at the shout in her mind. *Yes, Tamaak?*

The elder, who had always frightened her just a little even as she knew he was a kind and wise leader, had fixed her with an angry stare. *What is this? What have you been doing to the lieutenants Paris and Torres?*

N-nothing . . . . But one could not lie convincingly in a mental link.

He strode toward her, forcing the thoughts from her shield. Hot embarrassment and fear of Tamaak's reprisal coursed through her as he saw what she had been thinking, doing, and dreaming. His face grew first angry, then sad. Gently, to Priana's surprise, he placed a paw on her shoulder.

Oh, Priana . . . I thought you knew better than this.

So what if she has taken a fancy to Paris? interrupted Imraak. *He is an inferior species. If Priana wants to make him forget about this Torres and devote himself to her for the duration of this journey, why shouldn't she?*

Tamaak whirled. He opted for speech, so that even the weakest telepath among them could understand the full depth of his outrage. "For millennia, ever since our brains evolved to the point where we could read and send thoughts, we realized the invasion of free will this could pose," he growled, drawing himself up to his full height as he advanced on Imraak. "We respected the barriers of others. We do not probe their thoughts unless we are invited, we do not force our will on others—"

"And what are we doing on this ship right now?" retorted Imraak, also speaking aloud. "Are your morals so flexible that you can pick and choose exactly where and how you will exercise them?"

"That is a different situation, and you know it, Imraak! That is the goal of our people, our very race. This—this whim of Priana's is selfish and hurtful and I will not permit her to continue!"

Priana was mortified. She wished she could melt through the floor. She lowered her head and covered it with her arms, whimpering. All along, she had known it was wrong. But Paris was so appealing, even in his human ugliness, so sweet and clever and funny . . . and only that ridge-headed, sour-tempered engineer stood between them. It had been so easy. It was done almost before she realized it.

Suddenly pain ripped through her and she gasped. Her face felt like it was on fire. She groaned, sinking back on her powerful hindquarters as the agony shuddered through her. It was all she could do to erect a quick block against the onslaught of Tom's thoughts and think clearly herself.

All of the Skedans were staring at her now. Some of them looked pained themselves and she knew her thoughts had bled into theirs. She turned huge, wet eyes to Tamaak. *He is hurt. He might be dying. I must go to him!*

Before they could stop her she was out the door, her long, strong legs carrying her swiftly down the corridor. Her people followed her, crying for her to stop, but she ignored them. She reached the turbolift, stumbled inside and cried, "Sickbay!" They reached the door just as it was closing—too late to stop her.

Tom. Tom. I'm sorry. I'm coming . . . .

The door to sickbay hissed open and Torres entered. Her gaze scanned the room full of injured and found the one she had come to see. Her heart pounding, uncertain of her reception, she walked toward him.

He looked dreadful, but he'd be all right. It didn't appear that there was anything that a dermal regenerator wouldn't fix. She breathed a sigh of relief and the knot in her gut untied for an instant, than wrapped itself up again as someone else came in the door.

Priana scurried up to Tom's side, panting from exertion. She reached out a three-fingered paw as if to place it on Tom's hand.

"Don't you touch him," growled Torres.

The young female looked up and Torres recoiled from the naked agony in the youngster's eyes. "I'm sorry," breathed Priana. "It wasn't right."

As she gazed at the alien, Torres suddenly felt energized. Her mind was clear and focused, her body strong and relaxed. She wasn't angry at Tom. She wasn't even angry at Priana anymore. All she felt was a calmness, and in that pool of calm her love for Tom rose like a shimmering bubble to the surface.

When Priana did place her hand on Tom's, Torres didn't mind. A few seconds later he opened his eyes.

"B'Elanna," he rasped. "What happened? We were fighting the Ku—"

"From what I heard, the console exploded," said the Doctor, stepping in briskly and running a medical tricorder over Paris's injuries. "You're lucky to be alive, though I imagine it smarts like the dickens."

"Actually, it doesn't hurt at all," said Paris in a wondering tone.

The Doctor glanced at him. "Shock," he said knowingly. "Ladies, I'll have to ask you to leave. In case you hadn't noticed, there are many others wounded here besides our intrepid pilot. Shoo."

Torres and Priana obliged. As B'Elanna turned to go, Tom reached out a burned hand to her. She hesitated, then clasped it as gently as she could.

"Dinner tonight?"

Torres felt a smile curve her lips. "Sure. What's on the menu?"

"Nothing blackened or well done," he said and gave her a wink.

Torres permitted herself a chuckle. She felt good, despite the dire situation, better than she had for days. Whatever mood had been upon Tom, it had gone. There were no more clouds between them.

Priana touched his hand a last time. The Doctor, examining his tricorder, frowned.

"That's odd," he said. But he said it to himself; Torres and Priana had gone.

Annika/Seven found that nearly everything in Engineering was now familiar to her. She moved comfortably from console to console, assisting where needed and offering what help she could. The repairs were proceeding rapidly. Captain Janeway would be pleased.

At one point, the flowing red dress that had so appealed to her a few hours before snagged on a corner and tore. She frowned. A billowy dress might be comfortable, but it was not practical. Something more form-fitting was necessary to work efficiently in this environment.

The birds were still with her. Thirteen of them, sitting quietly on various pieces of equipment and regarding her with sharp eyes. She paused in her work to stare back at them for a moment.

The Doctor had said they weren't real, and certainly no one else could see them. They were, according to his thinking, part of her recovery from the hallucinations he assured her she had been having. At the moment, she couldn't remember them, but she'd witnessed recordings of herself deep in the throes of these other lives and knew that it had happened.

A bird . . . not a blackbird . . . It had spindly legs and scarlet-and-black plumage . . . .

"A skorrak," she breathed. "I remember . . . ."

Not a hallucination. A memory. She recalled it not

with the immediacy of living it, but with the softer, kinder haze of recollection. A true memory, as vivid and intact as recalling the battle with the Ku, or, as she knew them, the Tuktak, an hour or so ago on the bridge.

A smile curved her lips. This was a breakthrough, progress of a clear and definable sort. Perhaps she was finally starting to heal. She remembered Keela, remembered . . . .

Her brow furrowed in a frown. More memories of Keela, the young Graa female, floated back. Bad memories, memories of fear and capture and—

Annika/Seven's grip on the engineering tool tightened until her hand hurt. She was remembering being assimilated—not as Annika Hansen, but as Keela. Laid over this recollection of Keela's, like a thick layer of dust on an old piece of equipment, was her own memory, as Seven of Nine, Tertiary Adjunct of Unimatrix Zero-One.

It was the same scene. The assimilation of Keela, and Seven now saw it from both sides. She had been the Borg who had slain Keela's mother, who had lifted her mechanical gaze to the cowering kitten, uttered the terrifying words and forced her into the Collective.

And now, as if a gate had been flung open, other memories filled her mind's eye. The sculptor and elder Druana, facing down Seven of Nine with a calmness and integrity that was humbling. Seven had triumphed, of course. The Borg always did. The recollection from first Druana's perspective and then her own memory made Seven feel vaguely ill. Unaware of her movement, she put a hand on her stomach.

She had overseen the final stage of Amari's assimilation. Amari had unexpectedly awoken during the medical procedures. She, Seven, had felt nothing as she amputated Amari's arm. It was nothing to her, a Borg drone. It was part of the process, that was all, and if anything it was helping the pitiful, feathered creature named Amari attain the perfection the Borg Collective could offer—

Except, thanks to the memories of these people whose lives she had destroyed, Seven now realized what a violation she had been a part of. The destruction of the individual. She had heard and, to borrow a human phrase, rolled her eyes at Captain Janeway's ranting about how humans and other sentient beings would rather be dead than assimilated. Now, she realized that the captain was right.

She remembered what it was like to be a kitten chasing a bird in the warm sun, a woman in love with her betrothed, an elder with a gift for beauty, and a thousand thousand other lives that she, Seven of Nine, had emotionlessly destroyed in a heartbeat—

"What have I done?" she whispered. Her stomach churned and there was an ache in the center of her chest. She had experienced remorse for the first time over Kovan's suicide, but it was nothing compared to the shaky, sick feeling that overwhelmed her now.

A shadow fell across her. For a moment, Seven couldn't move. Finally, she forced herself to look up.

Standing over her was B'Elanna Torres, someone who had made no secret of her dislike for the former Borg. The two had clashed often enough and probably would in the future, but at this moment, Seven realized that the expression on the half-Klingon's face was concern.

"Are you all right?"

Slowly, Seven shook her head. "No," she whispered. "And I never will be again."

CHAPTER
14

HARRY COULDN'T THINK OF ANYTHING TO SAY AS HE walked beside Seven. All the sympathetic phrases, "It'll be all right," "I know what you're going through," seemed forced and stilted if not downright lies. He didn't know if she was going to be all right, and he certainly had no comprehension of what she was going through.

She should be in sickbay, but the Doctor had his hands full and had said so in no uncertain terms when Harry had escorted Seven there. And he was right—it was standing room only in sickbay after that last battle with the Ku.

The doctor had prescribed regeneration and then a

hearty meal, so here they were, heading back to her alcove in Cargo Bay Two. And Harry couldn't think of anything to say to ease her pain.

"She is no longer present," said Seven.

He glanced at her. "What? Who?"

"Annika Hansen." Seven lifted her gaze from the corridor floor and looked him in the eye for a second before again glancing down. "She was here for a time. She was all I was. But she has faded again."

Kim shrugged, totally at a loss. "Well . . . if you got your memories back from your time as Seven of Nine, of course you'd be more than just Annika Hansen."

"You do not understand." Her voice was sharp and there was a hint of something in it that Harry didn't recognize. "People liked her. They do not like me."

Oh, now he *did* know what to say. "Seven, that's not true and you know it. We all like you. You're part of the team."

Again the quick glance. The gesture was almost furtive. "I do not believe you, Ensign. I am disliked and feared. Perhaps I have earned a measure of respect because of my contributions. Perhaps not. I am Borg and no one can forget that. Not even I, not even for a full day."

"You *were* Borg," Kim corrected. "You're not anymore. You're Seven of Nine, someone unique and special."

She stopped and turned to face him. "You do not make a good liar, Ensign, so do not attempt a falsehood. You met Annika Hansen. Do you like me better than her?"

He felt his face grow hot. The answer was so much more than a simple yes or no, and he groped for words. A humorless smile curved her lips.

"It is as I suspected. I suppose I can see her appeal."

"Seven, you don't understand. Annika was more like us, more—we could relate to her. You're harder, more of a challenge to get to know. But that doesn't mean that you're not a good person even though you're calling yourself Seven of Nine and not Annika Hansen!"

"A good person." She considered the phrase. "Vague, yet restrictive. What is a good person, Ensign? Am I? Are you? Are the Skedans? The Tuktak?"

Her words were hard, like hammer blows, and Harry started to get angry. "You're quibbling over semantics here, Seven."

"And yet that is how you communicate. Should I not be, as you phrase it, quibbling over the finer nuances and shadings of your words?"

Harry frowned. "Now you're just trying to pick a fight. Well, I won't play that game." The cargo bay door hissed open. "I'm more than happy to talk with you about words, Seven. Heck, I'll talk with you about anything you like, whenever you like. You should know that by now. I'm your friend. But you're—you're not yourself and I'm afraid I'm just going to make things worse. There's your alcove. I'll check in with you in three hours and take you to the mess hall, all right?"

She stared at him, her expression unreadable. Then she nodded once, and stepped into the alcove. She straightened, adjusting her body to the proper position, and closed her eyes.

He watched her for a couple of minutes. He hadn't lied when he said she was someone unique and special. This whole ordeal had shaken her to her core and the rest of the crew had been rattled right along with her. He sighed, and went to return to the bridge.

Seven opened her eyes after hearing the door shut. Even such a simple movement felt difficult, as if her body were heavy and clumsy instead of strong and graceful. She preferred having her eyes open. When they were closed, it was as if the scenarios had been granted new life. She saw the murder of Keela's mother, the dismemberment of Amari, the anguish on the face of Rhiv as she cuddled her children close in a futile effort to protect them from the horror descending from the skies.

After Kovan's suicide, she had gone to the Doctor and requested that he remove the feeling she was experiencing. He had told her that he was not able to do so—that she'd have to learn to live with her remorse and that eventually it would subside. He had been correct. Kovan's untimely death had ceased to occupy her thoughts and she had, as the humans liked to put it, "gotten on with her life."

But this . . . Seven groaned and sank slowly to the floor, reaching out trembling hands to the walls of the alcove for support. The anguish she had caused. All those lives ruined because of her, because she had been Borg, because she was Borg, now and forever.

It could not be borne.

Her stomach roiled as the by-now familiar scent of rot surrounded her, but she forced herself to be calm. Frantic activity would not accomplish the desired results. She had to be effective to be successful.

Yes, thought Imraak. He had curled up in a corner of the cargo bay, wrapped in the poor rags that served as blankets. He had scorned Janeway's offer for better coverings, clinging to what little was left of his world. The children at play did not notice him, and the foolish Tamaak was deep in mental conversation with Shemaak. They were paying him no heed.

No living with this, is there, Seven? Such pain. Such dreadful suffering, and it's all your fault, all your fault . . . .

It was all her fault. And there was no way to atone for any of it. The complex concepts of compassion and forgiveness had eluded her every time she had attempted to grasp them. Seven thought in terms of efficiency, of logic, of balance, and there was no place for forgiveness in that kind of a system. And forgiving herself? How? She did not have the coping mechanisms, never had, never would.

But she could ensure that this would never again happen. And there was just one way to do that.

Seven of Nine rose and walked, unsteadily, around the cargo bay searching for tools that would suffice for this particular task. She met with frustration. Nothing was sharp enough. Finally, in exasperation, she began to seize various storage boxes and rummage through them. There were no knives, no weapons stored here. Only containers, and samples of—

Yes. A few months ago they had collected samples of a hitherto unknown geological formation. The rock was harder than any substance that was naturally encountered. The ancient natives of the planet had built domiciles out of it that lasted for centuries. Yet this stone, considered a gift from the deities of the planet and called "blessingstone," fragmented easily into jagged, sharp pieces when struck at precisely the right angle. Thus, the same stone was excellent for building nearly indestructible houses and for creating efficient weaponry.

Seven was unexpectedly nervous as she picked up the bright-blue blessingstone. She examined it, turning it this way and that. Which was the correct angle? The lighting in the cargo bay was poor. It helped her relax when she was regenerating, but now she wished it were better. She ran her fingers lightly over the stone, searching for the telltale "guiding fissure" the aliens had shown them.

Ah, there it was. Yes. One good blow from something solid would do it. She reached into the box and withdrew a second blessingstone, positioned it against the guiding fissure of the first, and then struck hard.

The blessingstone shattered into dozens of shards, each perfectly sized to be an ideal spearhead. It was no wonder the people thought the stones sacred.

Seven picked up one and stared at it. Now that the moment had come, she found that she was afraid. She lacked the courage to do what needed to be done.

Perhaps the humans were right. Perhaps there was forgiveness, even for someone like her.

No! thought Imraak, clutching the blanket. *The time for fooling yourself is gone. There can be no forgiveness for what you've done—only atonement. You must do it.*

No enduring it a moment longer.

There was no enduring this a moment longer. Seven grasped the stone in her left hand and turned her right hand palm up. The soft flesh of her wrist, unprotected by Borg technology, would part easily with a single stroke of the sharp stone. Harry would not check back for three hours. By then, it would be over.

Over.

She took a deep breath and pressed the stone to her wrist.

With a cacophonous chorus of shrieks, the ravens who had until now sat silently watching her exploded into action. They dove at her head, pecking furiously. Black wings hammered her face. Seven cried out and flung her hands up against the onslaught. Still they came, their beaks tearing chunks of flesh from her soft face and exposed hands. She huddled forward and felt blood trickling down her cheeks. It dripped into her lap, merging with the crimson of her dress.

Seven gritted her teeth. These birds of the mind were trying to stop her. She wouldn't let them. She knew what she had to do. For the second time she pressed the sharp edge of the blessingstone against her bare wrist.

"Don't!" came a voice, high with terror.

The birds disappeared.

Seven started and glanced up. Two yards away, staring at her with enormous eyes, was a little girl. Seven did not recognize her. To the best of her knowledge, there was only one child aboard *Voyager* and that was Naomi Wildmon. This was a human child, with long blond hair and wearing a frilly white dress.

"Please, don't," she said again, more softly. "I need you, Seven. Don't kill me."

Seven was vaguely aware that her flesh was intact, both at her wrist and where the birds had pecked her. The damage had vanished.

"Kill you? But—" Seven froze as comprehension crashed over her. She stared at the little girl, who stepped forward cautiously. For a long moment, they gazed at each other.

"Annika," breathed Seven. The girl nodded and a tremulous smile curved her lips.

"Don't kill us," she repeated. "You're afraid. You feel guilty. But you're all that's left of me, and I don't want to die!"

Deep inside, Seven knew this for what it was. Part of her was thinking clearly. Part of her did not want to die, regardless of the crashing wave of remorse that threatened to sweep away sense, sanity, and life itself. That part, manifested first in the black birds and now in the form of herself as an innocent child, was begging her to think, to hesitate just long enough to realize what she really wanted.

Seven of Nine wanted to live.

* * *

No! Imraak projected his thought with all the force of a physical blow. *No, you want to die! Living is intolerable. The little girl is being selfish. She doesn't understand.*

"You don't understand," rasped Seven of Nine. Tears were flowing down her cheeks and she dragged an arm across her wet face. "You don't know how awful it is . . . to live with this . . . ."

The child, her face wiser than her six years, nodded solemnly. "But I do know, Seven. I know everything. I remember being assimilated—and so do you. They took me, took us, and put us in a stasis chamber." Her child's mouth lisped over the words, but there was knowledge in her blue eyes. "They removed parts of our body and replaced them with cold metal. They made us do the same to others. You are free. You have a chance to embrace being an individual. Do you think that Keela would turn her back on such an opportunity?"

Startled, Seven thought of the small kitten. She couldn't imagine little Keela taking her own life. Nor proud, dignified Druana. Nor Rhiv, so full of life and love, nor Amari, fighting to the end.

"No," she said slowly. "I don't think she would."

"Then don't. Fight your pain." Annika moved closer to Seven until she was a hand's breadth away. She smelled clean, like fresh air and flowers, and the carrion scent fled before the fragrance. The scent made Seven's heart hurt. "Don't give in. Don't kill us."

Seven gasped as something deep inside her shattered. "I won't!" she sobbed, reaching out to fold the child into her arms. Annika hugged her tightly. Seven buried her face in the golden curls, breathed in the sweet, poignant little-girl scent. "I won't," she promised.

Behind Annika, wheeling and turning and cawing in delight, flew fourteen black birds.

And huddled in a corner of Cargo Bay One, Imraak, for only the second time in his life, tasted defeat.

CHAPTER
15

WHEN ENSIGN KIM ARRIVED PRECISELY THREE HOURS later, Seven was completely in control. She had shed her flowing red garment in favor of her customary brown unitard. Her hair had been brushed and re-pinned neatly in a coil at the back of her head. She noted and dismissed his reaction—a quick burst of dismay, an equally swift recovery and return to nor-malcy.

The peculiar and nearly lethal wave of despair that had flooded her earlier had been vanquished. She was slightly embarrassed by it now, and by her previous maudlin longing to be "liked." Being liked was irrele-vant. She was crisp and cool when Harry arrived and she hoped he, too, would think no more on their earlier conversation.

"Ready for some lunch?" he asked.

She considered the emptiness in her abdomen. "Yes," she confirmed. "I am hungry."

When they entered the mess hall, Neelix's homely face flooded with pleasure. "It's a pleasure to see you back here—" He hesitated.

She replied, "I am Seven of Nine."

"Ah. Just wanted to make sure. Always good to know who you're talking with, eh?" She noted that he seemed just as happy to receive Seven of Nine in his special culinary domain as he had been to feed Annika Hansen chocolate cake. "Come along. I checked in with the Doctor to see how you were doing and he told me I should plan on seeing you after you'd had a little time to regenerate. How are you feeling?"

She carefully considered the question. "I am well," she said finally. It was true enough. She hadn't felt this calm since the whole ordeal began. Now, if the fifteen black birds would only go away, she thought she could safely say that she was cured. The memories were floating back. Now she remembered that she had never had a particular fondness for Neelix's version of nutritional supplements and sat down at the table with a sense of trepidation.

"Seven," said Harry, still standing, "I've got to get back to my post. Are you—will you be okay?"

"Yes," she stated. "I will report to the Doctor after I have ingested my nutritional supplements. He has indicated that my brain has recovered sufficiently for him to attempt neural stimuli without risk of damage."

He smiled a little. "Yeah, you're going to be okay." He hesitated, seemed about to say something else, then left abruptly.

Neelix returned, his whiskers drooping with dismay. "Ensign Kim had to leave? What a pity. I've quite the gustatory experience lined up here today! All righty, we have tekkaberry muffins, fresh hot vegetable soup just loaded with nutrients," and here he winked at her, "and for dessert—your favorite. Chocolate cake!"

He lifted the napkin off the plate with a flourish. Seven noted the food items he had mentioned and something else—a small bowl of what looked to be seeds. She raised a questioning eyebrow.

"The birdseed is for your little friends," said Neelix.

Heat rushed over her and she felt the blood rise in her cheeks. "You are mocking me," she accused, her voice icy with indignation.

"Oh, no!" Neelix sat down in the chair beside her. "Not at all."

"Then you are humoring me. The birds do not exist," Seven continued. "Do not pretend that they do."

"But they do exist—in your mind," replied Neelix, tapping his mottled temple. "If you can see them, then they do have a reality—of a sort. The Doctor has said that he thinks these birds are an aspect of your subconscious trying to reassert itself, to tell you something. Have they told you anything yet, Seven?"

"No," she admitted.

"Maybe you need to be nice to them. Take care of them. Let them know they're important and that whatever they have to say, you're ready to listen. You know and I know that imaginary birds can't eat birdseed."

"Ravens need more than seeds for a balanced diet. They feed on small mammals, fruits, carrion—"

"Seven, Seven," interrupted Neelix, lifting his hands in gentle protest, "you're missing the point. Offer the birdseed as a gesture. That's all. You don't have to worry about feeding them a balanced diet."

She stared at the seeds in annoyance. "You sound like Commander Chakotay."

"Do I?" The little Talaxian sat up straighter. "Well! That's quite a compliment. Thank you!" He rose, beaming at her. "If you don't want to take me up on my suggestions, then just leave the seeds. I won't be offended." He bounced off, whistling cheerily.

Seven watched him go. Various emotions warred within her. The seed idea was childish. Foolish. And yet, she had to admit it made a certain amount of sense. But she was angry about it nonetheless.

She dove into her food with more duty than enthusiasm, chewing the muffins with their too-tart berries and spooning up soup crowded with unidentifiable vegetables. She saved the cake for last. The innocuous slice of pastry made her nervous. Chocolate cake was Annika's treat, not Seven's. She was tempted to just leave it and the birdseed, to let Neelix know what she, Seven of Nine, thought of his gestures.

But then she remembered the sweetness of the cake, the wonderful hit of chocolate on her tongue. Her heart beating rapidly, she carefully cut a piece with her fork and brought it to her lips. The sweet, sugary smell reached her nostrils, and when she put the bite in her mouth, she found that pleasure in this simple thing, at least, had not deserted her.

Seven took another bite, savoring the flavor, and wondered why there was suddenly a peculiar lump in her throat.

As he strode through the airy, exquisitely crafted corridors of the First Imperial Domicile, Xanarit was hard put to conceal his pleasure. Within the last turn he had received a message that to anyone else would sound like so much nonsense, but to him was the sweetest news in the world:

Little One to Big One. House here, it flies well. Torch on fire. Light results. Purple flower in bloom and the star is falling.

The translation, according to the code that Xanarit and his people had worked out, was: *Tatori government, via Elebon Boma, to the Iora. The water-extraction system is in place and is functioning well. We have enough water to save our people and to irrigate crops. The food shipment is being distributed and we are deeply in your debt.*

It had been a tense few days, but the apprehension had been worth it. The Iora, acting in secret and under the leadership of Xanarit, had saved millions of innocent Tatori lives. Even if Beytek had discovered the deception and ordered them executed—or worse, put a price on their heads for the Ku to claim—all the members of the Iora had determined that the risk was a worthy one.

Xanarit's greatest fear was that he would be intercepted before the supplies had been successfully delivered. There was still the chance that Beytek had stumbled onto the plot and was setting up this meeting to order to capture him, but that did not distress the council's leader. The only regret he had was that if the Iora's treason was discovered, they would be unable to continue to help those whom the Emperor had wronged.

Mintik, his Second, fell into step with him. He acknowledged her presence by dipping his head and flicking his black tongue. She returned the traditional greeting and they continued in silence.

Most of the eleven others had already assembled in the council chamber by the time Mintik and Xanarit entered. Formal greetings were exchanged, but otherwise the mood was silent and tense. Emperor Beytek, of course, would delay his entrance for the maximum impact.

They heard the Emperor long before he appeared. This time, he had brought his cadre of musicians with him, and their sprightly tunes carried through the halls. Xanarit and Mintik exchanged glances. For a brief instant Mintik's eyesacs flushed red, conveying her annoyance, then returned to their normal shade of purple.

One of Xanarit's tasks was to oversee the Emperor's personal expenditures. Not that he had any control over it, but it was one of the ritual duties of his stature as leader of the Iora. He knew that the amount earned by a single one of these musicians, who did nothing better with their great gifts than to dance merrily before their ruler while playing cheerful melodies, would have bought three hundred thousand *danos* of food for the starving Tatori populace. He felt his own blood rise at the obscenity of it, and had to quickly bring his emotions under control.

The music was loud now, and the first six musicians leaped into the room. They were indeed talented— the songs were lovely and in addition to playing music the performers did astonishing leaps, tucks, and rolls—but they were unnecessary, a frivolous expense incurred by a corrupt, careless ruler. The second six followed, followed by the third set. Eighteen was a sacred number to their people, and the Emperor liked to make sure that, when possible, he had eighteen of everything. Or eighteen sets of eighteen.

Beytek, as usual, was borne on his litter. A fatuous smile was on his scaly face and he waved and nodded languorously, as if the powerful, honored Iora were nothing more than a crowd at a celebratory parade. He was set down gently and assumed his traditional place, on the embroidered cushion on the highest tier. He fussed with his medallions, searched for the sweetest fruit, ate, helped himself to a goblet of *voor* wine and then, as if only now noticing his gathered advisory council, waved them to their own seats.

Xanarit gathered himself and opened his mouth to address the lengthy list of pressing issues. Beytek interrupted him before he could utter a single syllable.

"Have you implemented my orders from our last meeting, Xanarit? Has security been doubled on all of the waystations?"

Xanarit kept an expression of placid stupidity on his face. "Not quite doubled, O Great One, but we have increased the amount of—"

"Are your mathematics so poor that you do not understand when your god says doubled?" Angrily, Beytek picked up the bowl of fruits and hurled it down at Xanarit's head. The chief advisor barely leaped out of the way in time to avoid serious injury. The bowl had been carved from stone. Xanarit was more annoyed than fearful. This flinging of items at his head was becoming a habit with the Emperor.

"Had I merely wanted an increase, I would have said so. When I say doubled, I mean *twice as many as before!*"

Something is bothering him, thought Xanarit, suddenly on the alert. Anything that bothered the Emperor could only be good news to his chief advisor. For an instant, Xanarit wondered if Beytek was merely baiting him. He immediately dismissed the idea. Beytek was not capable of such subtlety. Had their plot been discovered, the guards would already have marched in and arrested them. They were safe, at least thus far. Something else—someone else, perhaps—had thwarted the Emperor, and Xanarit had a hunch he knew what—who—that was. Hope flickered inside him.

"As my lord demands," he replied, keeping his eyes lowered. "The orders are in place. It is only that it takes time to bring the people to the planets, O Great One."

The answer seemed to mollify Beytek. He grunted and scratched himself with a long black claw. "As long as they will be in place before Tribute."

"Most assuredly."

"Are my orders regarding Tribute being followed, or are you indulging in more creative mathematics?"

Xanarit nodded to Mintik, who rose. "I have been appointed to handle Tribute, O Great One. I am pleased to report that all is going as well as even Your Most Excellent Worthiness could wish. Every channel has been used to promote Tribute. We have contacted every planet in the Empire and they have all agreed to feature the vidfeed of the event as it unfolds. Many planets have moved to make Tribute a holiday on their worlds, as we have here on Lhiaari. All eyes will be upon you, O Great One, at the hour of your highest honor—when all worlds pay Tribute to Emperor Beytek Nak-Sur the Seventh!"

Beytek looked both surprised and pleased. He settled back on his cushion and his eyesacs inflated with self-satisfaction. "You all would do well to emulate Mintik. Keep pleasing me as you do, Mintik, and you may someday soon answer to Leader, not Second."

"An honor that His Most Eminent Worthiness will

see fit to bestow when and if it pleases him," murmured Mintik.

"This will be a most remarkable Tribute this year," Beytek continued. "Such recognition. Such honor. I cannot tell you how I am looking forward to it."

Xanarit regarded his leader with a face that revealed nothing.

Nor can I, Beytek, he thought, *nor can I.*

CHAPTER

16

"DO YOU KNOW WHAT TIME IT IS?" DEMANDED THE
Doctor as he materialized. He immediately answered
his own question. "It's 0327!" He yawned and rubbed
his eyes.

Seven frowned. "Doctor, you are a hologram. You
do not require sleep."

"True," he admitted. "Just practicing. It makes me
appear more human to the rest of the crew. Now,
what can I do for you . . . ." He hesitated. This was
becoming annoying.

"I am Seven of Nine," she stated. "Annika Hansen
has—has gone."

"Ah. That does put an end to the nomenclature

issue. You're late. You were supposed to report here directly after your meal." He caught sight of a small pouch fastened to her waist by a thong. "Doggie bag?"

"Birdseed." At his expression, she added hastily, "Neelix's suggestion. Do not inquire. After ingesting my meal I felt the need to work for a while, to—to think about things."

"Understandable." He waved her to the diagnostic bed and she lay down. The metal bridge closed over her torso. "How has your memory recovery been progressing?" he inquired in a cool, professional voice.

Seven took a deep, steadying breath and answered in a like manner. "I have a theory regarding the reason why the memories of Druana, Keela, and the others were so powerful—overwhelming, in fact. I believe it was due to the fact that I was the one who assimilated them."

His movements, assembling tools and analyzing the results of his medical tricorder, halted for an instant, then continued. "That makes sense. You encountered them under extremely traumatic circumstances, and in the normal process of your becoming more organic and less cybernetic, the memories manifested themselves."

"I now recall myself assimilating them, and their own experience of the same incident."

"Double memories. It must be confusing."

"It is simple enough to distinguish one from the other." She was quiet for a moment as he continued his examination. "I am fit to return to duty. I recall everything about the vessel now."

"You leave that to me. I'll make the determination about returning you to full duty. How about the birds?"

Sixteen of the black birds perched about the room. Seven sighed. "They are still present."

"Then I'm not returning you to duty."

"Doctor—"

"Seven of Nine," said the doctor in a strict tone—*Annika Hansen, you put that down right away*—"I am not about to pronounce a crewman who hallucinates—how many birds?"

"Sixteen."

"Sixteen birds as fit for active duty. You may continue to work in a limited capacity." He frowned over his tricorder. "Sixteen. You must be close to a murder by now."

Seven started. *"What?"*

He glanced up briefly, and repeated the word, exaggerating the pronunciation. "Mur-der."

"I find it unsettling that you think my mental situation may deteriorate into such a dangerous psychosis," she said.

"What? Oh. No, Seven, you misunderstood. In English, the term for a grouping of crows is a murder. Although your birds are probably ravens, so it would be an unkindness."

"It would be unkind to refer to them as crows?"

He glared at her. "An unkindness of ravens. Much the way we discuss a pack of wolves, a flock of sheep, a gaggle of geese, a squabble of Klingons." He smiled. "Klingon gatherings aren't actually called 'squabbles,' of course. Though it would be an appropriate term.

Peculiar language, English. The Bolian native tongue is so much simpler—but then, so are Bolians. If you wish to categorize a group of anything in the Bolian tongue, all you need to do is—"

"Doctor!"

"Sorry. Just sharpening my rapier wit." He again turned his eyes to his instruments, and when he again spoke he was all business. "Considering how intense your experience has been, you are making a most impressive recovery. I'm still not sure what triggered your flashbacks—your suppressed memories from other sources, I should say—but you appear to have come to grips with them."

He ran the tricorder over her, narrowing his brown eyes as he analyzed the results. "Blood pressure normal, adrenaline level only slightly elevated, peptides elevated. The circuit through your amygdala and thalamus is very active still. Your limbic system is getting quite a workout. Now, I'm going to apply a controlled electric current to stimulate various parts of your brain. The levels I'll be using are perfectly safe, but they might help jog your memories. Tell me if they do."

Peptides. Limbic system. Amygdala. Seven frowned slightly. A memory stirred, but vanished before she could quite grasp it.

The doctor didn't miss it. "A recollection of something?"

She nodded. "Vague. What you are discussing with me sounds familiar."

"Probably because it's the same information that I've droned every time you've come in here."

Seven didn't think so, but she held her tongue. The memory would come back.

Over the next several minutes, Seven's mind gave her images she had forgotten. The agony of her first few hours of separation from the Collective. A toy she had been given on her fourth birthday. A fragment of a nursery rhyme about rings, roses, and falling down. Nothing of import, but vivid and real memories just the same.

As each one occurred, she described it for the Doctor. He nodded and recorded the information. Finally he sighed. "That's enough for one session. How do you feel?"

"A little tired."

"That's to be expected. Seven . . . I have a question." She nodded, indicating that he might proceed. "Did you assimilate the Skedans? Not you personally, but—"

"Yes. Personally. I have experienced the memories of one Rhiv, Species 4774. Known as the Skedans. A race of telepaths with a protective ridge of bone on the skull that protrudes down the back. Non-aggressive. Resistance was minimal. The young are inefficiently nurtured—"

"Telepaths? That would explain it. I noticed that their young ones emitted certain measurable bursts of mental energy and there's an extra organ in their brains. Tamaak said it was just a species anomaly. I wonder why he didn't let us know they were telepaths."

Seven searched Rhiv's memories. "They had been met with fear by non-telepaths in the past. They do not often exert their will on others. They have a highly detailed code of ethics involving mental contact with other species, divided into forty-eight—"

"That will do, Seven. Thank you. Come back in twenty-four hours and we'll continue our work. If anything out of the ordinary happens, contact me at once."

"Shall I return to duty?"

"No. You won't be thinking as clearly as you ought to, after this. Why don't you return to your alcove and regenerate?"

"I have done so within the last few hours. I wish to work."

"Then stay in Astrometrics. You can't do too much damage there."

Seven stood at her console, efficiently tapping in information and watching as the computer changed its images according to the new directives. Normally, the intricate maps she constructed pleased and interested her. Tonight, though, she found no satisfaction in the work.

Her mind kept drifting. She thought of Keela, and Rhiv—Rhiv who had been paired with Tamaak Vriis, who was here on this vessel. Perhaps that was why she had done what she could to avoid interaction with the Skedans.

The birds were a nuisance. They fluttered, hopped about, squawked, picked on one another, and generally distracted her. She remembered Neelix's pouch and reached to touch it.

Instantly the birds froze. As one, they turned to stare at her, expectant.

Her heart sped up. This was foolish. Offering birdseed to fictitious birds. And yet—

She licked her lips and spoke. "The Doctor says you are a part of me. Neelix thinks that you have things to tell me. I—I will listen. I will take care of you. Here."

Seven poured the contents of the bag into her hand, knelt, and made a small pile of birdseed on the floor. Then she rose and stepped back, waiting—for what?

For a long moment, the birds didn't move. Then, by ones and twos, they hopped forward and began to peck at the seed. They ate, and yet the pile was not diminished. Finally, they seemed satisfied and regarded her with sharp yellow eyes.

A sudden pain throbbed in Seven's temple. She groaned, involuntarily, and pressed her fingers to her head. The pain increased. She slitted her eyes against a bright light that appeared from nowhere, a light that she knew existed only in her troubled, hyperstimulated mind.

A murder of crows. An unkindness of ravens.

Unkindness.

Murder.

Sing a song of sixpence, a pocket full of rye; four and twenty blackbirds baked in a pie. When the pie was opened, the birds began to sing. Wasn't that a tasty dish to set before the king?

She began to breathe, rapidly and shallowly. Like a puzzle, the pieces were now all here. She had only to put them together. She glanced over at the birds, who had not moved.

Unkindness. Murder.

The last line of the song, the line she had somehow never been able to recall before. *Wasn't that a tasty dish to set before the king?*

"Unkindness," she rasped, as understanding burst over her. "Murder."

The world began to grow gray around the edges and she was aware that she was about to pass out from lack of oxygen. She forced herself to breathe deeply and slowly. The haze went away. Her mind clear, she gazed searchingly at the ravens, then, despite the earliness of the hour, pressed her commbadge.

"Seven of Nine to Captain Janeway."

A pause, then: "Seven? What's wrong? Are you all right?"

Her lips curved in a smile. "I am well, Captain, but I have some urgent information. I believe that the Skedans are using us to transport them to Lhiaari so that they can murder the Emperor."

CHAPTER
17

SEVEN WAS ALREADY IN SICKBAY, PER HER CAPTAIN'S orders, when Janeway entered. Janeway looked tired, Seven observed, but her body was taut with anger. The Doctor nodded in acknowledgment, but continued his adjustments on Seven's implants.

"There are times when I work with you, Seven, that I feel like Mr. Paris tinkering with his '69 Camaro," he muttered. "Good morning, Captain."

"Status report?" Janeway demanded, ignoring all pleasantries.

"I've almost completed—" the Doctor began, but Seven interrupted him.

"You need to monitor the activity of the neurotransmitters in the captain's brain," she said. "Until the Doctor finishes his adjustments to my implants, I will not be able to tell if the Skedans are monitoring your thoughts. Because of the hour, I do not think so, but we cannot be sure."

"Seven, what's all this about?" demanded Janeway. "You wake me up in the middle of the night, with some vague theory that the Skedans are plotting an assassination—"

"They are," replied Seven calmly. "I am certain of it."

"How do you know?"

"A little bird told her," said the Doctor. "Actually, seventeen birds, and they aren't quite so little. Seriously, Captain, I have evidence of my own that will support her theory. If I may?"

Janeway searched Seven's eyes, then nodded. Nimbly the Doctor affixed a small neural monitor to Janeway's temple and quickly ran a tricorder over it. He nodded. "I detect no unusual activity. You're clean, Captain."

"Now," said Janeway slowly, "I want an explanation, and I want it fast."

"As the Doctor has told you," said Seven, "I have been reliving the experiences of people I have assimilated. One of these was Rhiv, the lifemate of Tamaak Vriis. As my memory has returned, I now recall that the Skedans are powerful telepaths. The Borg decimated their planet. We assimilated millions and utilized their telepathic skills to enhance our own biological and technological distinctiveness. From what I am learning about non-Borgs, it would be natural for the Skedans to harbor a great deal of resentment toward the Borg. Especially for Tamaak Vriis."

"I follow you," said Janeway, nodding. "You're saying that you believe that these memory flashbacks of other lives were caused by the Skedans? To punish you?"

"There appears to be no other reason," put in the Doctor. "One can't completely rule out spontaneous memory recall, of course, as we have learned. Coincidences do happen. But the fact that there is a race of telepaths on this ship who have cause to hate the Borg—one of them very personally—does seem to be a bit too much of a coincidence. Especially as these memories were very wrenching for Seven to experience. Sounds like revenge to me."

"It would also explain the ease with which they were able to get us through all that red tape," said Janeway. "Seven, I'm sorry you had to go through all that."

"It is irrelevant," Seven replied. "What is more to the point is the fact that they seem to be influencing the minds of others on *Voyager* as well."

"What?" Janeway turned to the Doctor. "Can you confirm this?"

"I can," replied the Doctor grimly. "Seven has told me how the Skedans use their telepathy. Their brains have developed an extra section that I've never seen in any other race. This organ gives off electrical impulses, in much the same fashion as neurons.

Except the Skedans can direct and control what kind of electrical impulses they emit. Not only among themselves, but among other species as well."

"Let me see if I remember my Academy classes," said Janeway. "This electrical impulse propagates a signal in one neuron, and a chemical process transmits the signal to another or to a muscle cell, right? So, if the Skedans send an artificial stimulus to another person's neuron, the body and brain think that it's just a naturally occurring impulse."

"Correct," approved the Doctor. "Perhaps you should be my assistant instead of Mr. Paris. The Skedans could make you dance, smack yourself in the head, or imagine that you are lying in a spring meadow if they want."

"It is easily countered among the Borg," said Seven. "A simple adjustment prevents our neurons from receiving external signals. Unassimilated beings are not so fortunate."

"There is one clue that is unmistakable," said the Doctor. "And as far as Seven knows, the Skedans aren't able to control this. When they send out a signal to another brain, they inadvertently activate the olfactory system. The receptor of the impulse smells their favorite scent if the Skedans are attempting to make the experience pleasant, a foul odor if they wish it to be unpleasant."

"Fresh brewed coffee," said Janeway, softly. "When I first met Tamaak Vriis, I could have sworn I smelled freshly brewed coffee." She smiled sadly. "I thought it was just wishful thinking."

"In contrast," said Seven evenly, "I smelled carrion."

"If I had been a mere human," said the Doctor, rather smugly, "I would have been fooled, too. I would never have noticed the electrical impulses the Skedan children were emitting—they wouldn't have let me read my instruments correctly. Apparently, mastery of telepathy to the point where the impulses can be controlled comes with adulthood."

"I believe that we have a group of telepaths on board, and I believe they've been manipulating our minds—and, in the case of Seven, to the point of torture," said Janeway. "I can see where they'd resent her, but why us?"

Seven hesitated before replying. "As I said, I have reason to believe that their goal is to kill the Emperor. They were almost totally defenseless when the Borg came upon them. Perhaps they hold him responsible for their planet's destruction. When the Doctor completes his adjustments, I should be able to home in on any weapons they might be carrying."

"But we checked them for—" Janeway stopped in mid-sentence. "Damn. I bet the security guards smelled something really nice when they checked the Skedan packs. Seven, thank you. I've got enough to get Tuvok on it. Doctor, continue. When Seven's adjustments are done, let me know at once."

"I told you," said Tamaak, his large eyes pleading with her, "We are doubly victims—of the Scarlet Death and of prejudice."

Now that she knew what to look for—or, rather, sniff for—Janeway could easily detect the rich scent of fresh coffee.

"I smell coffee," she said, her voice hard. "That's my favorite smell in the universe. Tell me, what did Mr. Paris smell? Or my security guards? Your attempt to destroy Seven of Nine failed and she's recovered her memories. All of them, including knowledge of your telepathic skills. She'll be joining us shortly, Borg technology and all, and you may be able to make me think or see what you want, but you won't be able to fool her. Just as you weren't able to fool the Doctor," she added.

All the wind went out of Tamaak's sails. He literally seemed to grow smaller before her eyes. The smell of coffee faded. "I deeply regret the necessity of lying to you, Captain. Please believe that."

"But why, Tamaak? Seven has an idea, but I want to hear your side of the story."

"We had to get to Lhiaari. We knew the Ku were after us. We needed your protection. It is—it is all we have left, now."

"What is?"

He lifted his eyes and her heart sped up at the anger and pain in their brown depths. "Revenge, Captain. Revenge. You have spoken to me of your Federation of Planets. It broke my heart to hear of such loyalty among such diverse worlds. We paid Tribute every single year to the Emperor. We sent our telepaths to do his errands, despite the danger and the hatred that they faced from all the other races in the Empire. We did our part, and when we learned the Borg were descending upon our helpless planet, we had faith that Emperor Beytek would do his. There are no words—please, let me—"

He leaned forward, but that ancient enemy, fear, flared up in Janeway. She didn't dare let him try to manipulate her mind again. Once burned, twice shy.

"No," she said, shortly. "We communicate with words. Find them."

"As you wish. Though they are poor things, compared to the sharing of thoughts. You are familiar with the Borg, Captain. We had been promised five hundred vessels of war. Fearsome things that would make even Borg think twice. But they never came. The Borg ravished our world, assimilating millions. They carved huge scars upon our planet, stealing our technology. My—my mate, my children—they are either dead or serving the Collective with the skills of their minds. It is an abomination, Captain. But worse than the Borg, who never pretended to be other than the monsters they are, was the Emperor who vowed to protect his children and, in the epitome of cowardice, never came."

"Tamaak," said Janeway, gently.

"No. There is more. Perhaps he was afraid to fight, to reveal his strength, to draw attention to his precious homeworld. I cannot condone that, but I can understand it. But after the Borg had all but destroyed us, no succor came from the Empire. We learned that Beytek had been spreading lies—telling the Empire's subjects that our planet had been devastated by plague. No one was to go near it. No one was to have contact with Skeda or her people. And then—and then the Ku came, on the orders of Beytek, trying to finish what the Borg had begun. You see, he couldn't let the rest of his Empire know. We had to be silenced—all of us. Forever."

Janeway smelled no heavenly aromas. Tamaak might be lying yet, but this pathetic tale of attempted genocide had the ring of truth and anger to it. She stayed silent, sympathy showing in her eyes.

"We fled. Only one group escaped them—my group. We have been refugees ever since. Once, we had a solemn charter regarding the use of our mental powers to influence others, but need has forced our hands. We must get to Lhiaari, and reveal the dreadful cowardice of the being who rules over ninety worlds. The truth of what he did to us must be known!"

"I believe you," said Janeway. "And when we reach Lhiaari, I will speak to the Emperor and his advisory council about restitution. Our people believe in righting wrongs just as yours do, but not by violence."

Tamaak shook his head. "No. That is not enough. Beytek must be punished, Captain. Surely you see that! Please tell me you understand!"

"I do," she assured him. "With all my heart, I do. But I cannot condone this, Tamaak. Judging by their love of red tape, I'm willing to bet the Lhiaarians have a complex legal system, ways to punish those who commit crimes. If the Emperor has done all that you say, then let's expose him to the Iora and let him be tried in a court of Lhiaarian law. Let him answer to his people for what he has done."

"Tried?" Tamaak leaped to his feet. "He is a god,

Captain! You cannot try a god! But you can destroy one, and that is what we intend to do. Help us, I beg you, or at the very least, do not interfere."

"Sickbay to Janeway."

"Go ahead."

"Seven's implants have been adjusted. She's located the Skedan weapon."

CHAPTER
18

SEVEN OF NINE STRODE DOWN THE CORRIDOR. HER HAND held a phaser, set, by Janeway's orders, on stun. Her head was high, her whole mind and being focused on the task at hand. Behind her, seen only in her peripheral vision, flew eighteen black birds. Quite the crowd, now.

Quite the unkindness . . . .

Despite their presence, which probably meant that there were still unresolved issues lurking in her subconscious, Seven felt more herself than she had since first encountering the Skedans. She knew her enemy, finally. Now that the Doctor had adjusted her implants, they could no longer harm her by manipulating her mind, making her see and smell and feel things that were not there.

Seven was furious at the intrusion into her private thoughts. She remembered the feel of the blessing-stone's sharp edge against the soft, fragile skin of her inner wrist and had to repress a shudder. What if the birds had not distracted her?

What if Annika had not been more sensible, harder to reach and toy with, than Seven of Nine?

But there was no point in what-ifs. Disaster had not happened, and she, Seven of Nine, was in control.

It felt . . . good.

The two security guards Janeway had posted at the entrance to the cargo bay door nodded as she arrived.

"Captain Janeway has briefed you on the situation?"

"Yes," replied Ramirez. His face was creased in a frown. Seven detected rapid breathing. That and the way he held his body indicated anger.

"You were among the victims of the Skedans?"

He didn't meet her steely gaze. "I was one of the ones assigned to search through their things. I must have gone right past—whatever this weapon is and not even noticed it."

"Do not berate yourself. You were not aware the Skedans were telepaths. Even if you had been, and knew that your mind was being manipulated, it would have been impossible to see anything they did not wish you to see."

He shifted his weight. "Still—"

"Attaching blame where there is none is inefficient and illogical," she said crisply, forestalling his comment. "Now. I will be unaffected by their telepathic attacks. Are your weapons on stun?"

"Of course," replied Ramirez.

"Good. Then if the Skedans trick you into shooting one another, there will be no lasting harm done."

She ignored his glare and stepped inside.

Tamaak Vriis was still with Captain Janeway, but the other Skedans turned to look at her inquiringly. She noticed a few of them reacted when they realized it was she—the woman they had been deliberately, subtly attacking over the last several days.

"Any attempt at controlling my thoughts will be ineffective," she stated. "I have fully recovered my memories and have adjusted my implants accordingly. I suggest you surrender and turn over your weapon immediately."

They exchanged glances. One of them, Imraak, stepped forward. "What do you mean?" he asked, the very picture of innocence.

"It is foolish to continue the pretense," she snapped. "If you will not cooperate, I will search through your belongings myself. Starfleet protocol dictated that I present you with the option of compliance, but it is not necessary."

She could sense it. Once the Doctor had completed his task, she had immediately recognized the unmistakable energy signature that anything connected with Skedan mental energies emitted. It was in a pile of sacks in the corner. Without another word she moved toward it.

Imraak launched himself with a savage snarl. The impact of his compact, lean-muscled body sent her sprawling. Anger warred with fear—she should have expected this. The guards continued to stand at the entrance to the door, looking sullen. They saw nothing. Imraak didn't want them to.

With a grunt, Seven summoned her strength and rolled over. His claws slashed at her face, tearing the flesh. Pain crashed through her as she tried to free her hand from beneath his heavy body. The pinned hand still clutched the phaser, even though her long fingers were being crushed by Imraak's heavy body.

"It would have been easier had you died when I told you," he hissed in her ear. His jaws yawned open, and only by straining her entire body could Seven keep the sharp teeth from crunching down on her throat.

Then suddenly the weight was gone. She gasped, sliding backward and scrambling to her feet. Two others, females, one a mature adult, the other in the adolescent years, held Imraak firmly. Their strength was equal to his and he could not hope to break free from the two of them.

"Shemaak! Priana! Let me go—don't you see, she'll ruin everything—"

"I heard your words," snarled the one called Shemaak. "You tried to force her to take her own life. That is barbaric! Such a flagrant violation of everything we hold dear—"

"We've done enough to them," sobbed the younger one. "And I thought I had transgressed!" She turned an anguished visage up to Seven of Nine. "I'm sorry. I'm sorry. Perhaps this wasn't meant to happen after all. You'll find the weapon at the bottom of the pile."

"Priana! *Traitor!*" cried Imraak, still struggling. The eyes he turned up to his young captor were filled with raw hatred.

"She'd find it anyway," said Priana.

"Your young one is correct," said Seven. She had recovered herself and now knelt beside the pile. The energy signature was powerful now. Quickly she went through the sacks until she located a glowing sphere. She was reminded of the crystal balls of Earth's legends from tales Harry had told her—orbs in which one could see the future or the past, if one had certain gifts.

She had a gift. It was called an implant.

Seven touched her commbadge. "Seven to Captain Janeway."

"Janeway here."

"I have recovered the weapon."

"Excellent. What kind of weapon is it?"

Seven frowned. Before her, held in her hands, the sphere radiated energy and a soft, cool blue light. She had a gift which had allowed her to find it, but the skills of the Skedans were still superior. They had done something to the orb to prevent her from conducting a deep scan.

"I do not know," she said, and the thought irritated her.

Several hours later, after they had run every scan they could think of and a few others they had come up with on the spur of the moment, they still didn't know. And Seven was still irritated.

"I do not recall that the Skedans fashioned any weapon of this sort," she told Janeway. "This must be new technology."

"Or a twist on some kind of old technology," said the captain, staring at the orb on the console in sickbay. "Tuvok, any thoughts?"

"None," replied Tuvok. "The energy field that surrounds the orb is impenetrable. I have even attempted to mind meld with it, on the theory that perhaps something organic is housed within. But I have detected nothing. However," he added, with a lift of his eyebrow, "that does not mean that there is nothing inside to find."

"Clearly not," said Janeway. "I'm tempted to just beam it out into space, but without knowing exactly how it operates, the transporter could inadvertently trigger it." She tapped her commbadge. "Doctor, how is your security stint progressing? Any incidents?"

"Negative," growled the Doctor, his annoyance manifest even over the link. Because he and Seven were the only crew members who were certain to not be manipulated by the Skedans, Janeway had temporarily pressed him into a security role. He was presently stationed outside of Cargo Bay One, guarding all the Skedans inside.

"Quiet as a tomb. Captain, are you certain that I couldn't be more effective to you in my normal, intended, carefully designed capacity as a doctor?"

"Quite certain," and a smile curved her lips despite the tension of the moment. "Only you can ensure that our guests stay put. They're intelligent and inventive. They'd figure out some way to trick regular security personnel into deactivating the force field. I want you to bring Tamaak Vriis to sickbay. We've got some questions for him."

Janeway gazed a moment longer at the glowing sphere. "It's beautiful, isn't it?"

"Beauty is irrelevant," said Seven of Nine.

"I must concur," said Tuvok.

Janeway gave them both a wry grin. "Wet blankets, the both of you. But regardless of its beauty, you must admit it's amazing to think that the Skedans have the ability to create an energy field around an object simply with the power of their minds."

"It is," said Tuvok, somewhat reluctantly, "fascinating."

There was a hum. All of them turned to see the shape of Tamaak materializing in sickbay. Seven was surprised, then realized what the Doctor had done. An intraship transport would ensure that their reluctant "guest" would arrive where and when he was supposed to.

Tamaak looked—deflated. He stepped forward, his whole body crying defeat. "You wished to see me, Captain."

"I did." Janeway pointed to the orb. "Tell me about this weapon, how it functions, what its impact would be."

Tamaak lifted a slender head on a long neck and regarded Janeway impassively. "I regret it, but I cannot oblige you, Captain Janeway. Priana and Shemaak were right to stop Imraak from injuring you, Seven of Nine. I am sorry for what we put you through. Please believe me when I say I had no idea that Imraak had sent such—such evil instructions. I am glad you had the strength of will to resist. I have no desire to hurt or kill any of your crew, Captain. But I will not help you. Our ultimate purpose for surviving this long, for coming all this way, must be honored."

Janeway's patience had clearly worn thin. "You know I grieve for your people. You know I abhor what the Emperor did. And I will keep my promise—to bring this crime to light so that Beytek will be judged. But I won't sanction the killing of innocents."

Tamaak's expression was unreadable. "We all must follow our own paths, Captain." And that was all he would say on the matter.

"So," said Janeway, "I can't trust you, then, can I?"

Tamaak Vriis, leader of a dying people, victim of treachery and Seven of Nine's personal tormentor, looked her squarely in the eye.

"No," he said, softly. "In every sense of the word."

CHAPTER

19

CHAOS REIGNED IN THE IMPERIAL DOMICILE. IT WAS THE
Day of Tribute and Xanarit could barely squeeze past
the throngs of security, entertainers, petitioners, and
other assorted visitors en route to his meeting with
the Iora and Beytek. Thousands had come and filled
the streets to overflowing.

Xanarit was nervous, and his traitorous eyesacs
betrayed that nervousness. Fortunately, if anyone
noticed it, it would be attributed to the normal
excitement the day usually engendered. Still, he
wished his people did not possess such a telltale sign
of their emotions.

The guards nodded and waved him past each level

until he had reached the private "inner sanctum" of rooms reserved for the Iora and the Emperor. He breathed a deep sigh; the press of people had added to his agitation.

As usual, all the members of the Iora had assembled before the Emperor deigned to grace them with his divine presence, despite the delays in reaching the Imperial Domicile. The by-now familiar sound of the musicians heralded his approach, and Xanarit bowed his head respectfully with the rest as his Emperor entered and ascended to his perch.

For once, though, the Emperor did not partake of the sweets and fruits provided for his refreshment. He ignored them utterly, and gazed benevolently down at his advisory council as might a father regarding favored children.

"You have served me well, my Iora," he said, beaming. The members of the group so lauded shifted their weight and cast uneasy glances among themselves. Emperor Beytek *never* praised them, except on the rarest of occasions, and only then when his ego had been stroked. This unsolicited enthusiasm was unprecedented.

"Today is Tribute. The most wonderful holiday in the Empire, where every inhabited world shows how pleased they are to be considered a part of the Lhiaarian Empire—the greatest empire in the galaxy. All of my plans, carried out by you, my dear and hardworking Mintik, are coming to fruition in the happiest fashion possible. Come, Second, rise and acknowledge your worth!"

Xanarit's Second rose at her Emperor's command and bowed.

"Excellent. But!" And Beytek pointed a clawed finger up in a chastising gesture. "But, there are many things going on that you do not know about, could not know about."

Xanarit rose. "O Great One," he began, "we are your Iora—your advisory council. According to the charter which your illustrious ancestor Beytek the Second drew up at our founding, we must be notified of all activities and assist in coordinating them."

"In those simpler times, yes, Beytek the Second showed great wisdom in having a central council to organize and coordinate activities," Beytek agreed smoothly. His very placidness unnerved Xanarit still more. "But in these times—oh, how complicated the universe has become. We have gone beyond a single planet to ninety-six! We are coming close to ruling the quadrant—it will happen under my reign!"

Hardly, thought Xanarit, but kept silent.

"There are far too many complications for the Iora to know *everything,* hmmm? I am certain you agree with me, Xanarit—don't you?"

Xanarit knew a threat when he heard one and dipped his head in feigned subservience. "Of course, Your Most Excellent Worthiness."

"But the time has arrived to share the knowledge, much as the worlds share their wealth with the Emperor who has brought it to them." He thumped his tail down on the pillows three times and the doors opened.

It took every ounce of discipline Xanarit possessed not to cry aloud. As it was, he averted his head quickly so that Beytek would not see the sudden change of hue in his eyesacs.

Three guards led a prisoner into the council chamber. The prisoner, a bipedal creature with little hair save on its head, two eyes, unthreatening teeth, and unclawed hands, had been severely beaten. His torso was covered with welts and bruises. He was alive, but only just.

Xanarit knew him. The prisoner was Elebon Boma, the elected leader of the drought-stricken planet of Tatori. It was with him that Xanarit had discussed smuggling water-extraction systems. He was the one who had sent the message that had let Xanarit know that the system had been received and was functioning perfectly, that there was food to feed the starving on Tatori.

He knows! Xanarit's thoughts were a raw cry to which he could not give proper voice. *But how much does he know?*

"Foolish Elebon," said Beytek in a voice dripping with false pity. "He thought he could get away with not sending Tribute. He thought he could go behind my back—*behind the back of his Emperor!*—and contrive to get through other means what he had officially been denied. Behold the mercy of Beytek."

In a surprisingly graceful move for one normally so loath to indulge in physical activity, Beytek leaped from his perch to the floor with a soft thump. He poked at the prisoner and touched his face with an obsidian claw.

"I did not order him killed. I did not take reprisals against his family, as is my right. I merely asked him to reveal the names of his fellow traitors. But the fool has stayed silent."

Xanarit stared. Grief and rage racked him, but he did not dare speak. Once words began flowing off his tongue, he was not certain he could control them. Elebon had to know that he would most certainly die if he did not reveal what Beytek wanted to know, but he was the truest and the best of patriots. He would rather go to his death than trade his life for another's.

Beytek growled and slashed Elebon's face. Four deep cuts wept blood. Elebon did not utter a sound.

"Take him away. Keep . . . persuading him."

Mercifully, the dreadful sight of the bloodied but defiant Elebon was removed from Xanarit's view. The Iora was still safe, thanks to Elebon's courage. And if they were safe, then the plan could proceed.

"Xanarit, are you not glad now that I was wiser than you? I knew these Tatori were not worth troubling ourselves over. And you see now that I was right." He had returned to his cushion and now stared smugly down at Xanarit.

Xanarit found his voice. "The Emperor is always right," he managed.

"Of course. This was a sad thing to have to show you, but a triumph for the Empire in that we discovered Elebon's treachery and will eventually find out who aided him. On a happier note, I wish to present someone out of the tales of old—a legend come to life, that none of you have ever been lucky enough to meet until now."

Again the doors opened. The being that came forward was as different from poor, brutalized Elebon Boma as night from day. It scuttled forward on too many legs, looked at the assembled Iora with too many eyes.

"May I present Kraa T'Krr, the head of the Ku."

Kraa's hideous head swiveled, the multiple eyes focusing on each member of the Iora in turn. He lifted the upper part of his body and settled back on large rear appendages. Xanarit felt as though he were living a nightmare. The rumors of the Ku, dreadful though they were, had not prepared him for the obscene reality. They were giant insects, motivated only by hatred and a desire to kill beings whose blood ran warm in their veins. For a brief, shameful moment, Xanarit was intensely grateful that his people were reptilian.

"Don't pretend you haven't heard the tales," chided Beytek. "Everyone has. And here he is, standing before you. The time has come to bring all my arms into synch, Kraa. Please inform the Iora of your mission—and its pending success."

Black, shiny antennae waved in response. Kraa's mandibles opened and closed and his body began to vibrate, moving in a series of jerks and poses. *Like the tariflies that communicate where the nectar upon which they feed is located,* thought Xanarit, swallowing his disgust and horror.

The ornate translating mechanisms that the Iora and the Emperor wore as necklaces about their thick throats translated the bizarre dance-click words.

"His Most Excellent Worthiness Beytek the Seventh sent us on a mission of honor and glory," "said" Kraa. "The disgusting Skedans rose from the ashes of their world and flaunted their lives. Such a revelation could not be borne. His Most Excellent Worthiness sent us, the Ku, Killers of the Warms, Destroyers of the Foul, Slayers of those who are not holy, to end the wretched lives of the Skedans swiftly and with great delight. But the evil things had allies, fellow Warms who are ferrying them away from the skilled Ku. Our ships, never before harmed, were destroyed. Wicked, wicked, to know our secrets thus!"

The translator emitted a shrill sound of anger, apparently untranslatable. Xanarit winced at the volume. Kraa continued.

"We are in pursuit, only to find that they are coming here, as if making a gift of themselves and their passengers to the Emperor!"

Xanarit found it difficult to breathe. It was all falling apart, right before his eyes. His plan was about to fail, all because of a foolish, selfish emperor and his loathsome, hate-filled assassins.

"A gift indeed," said Beytek. "Here is what will happen."

CHAPTER
20

CAPTAIN'S LOG, SUPPLEMENTAL. SEVEN OF NINE APPEARS
*to be fully recovered, with the exception of the birds—
now about twenty—who seem to be her constant
companions. Thanks to her knowledge about the Skedans, we have been able to take appropriate measures
to contain them. The Doctor may not be enjoying his
new assignment, but he's the only hologram for the job.*

*We have still not been able to determine the nature of
the Skedans' weapon. Tamaak Vriis has assured me—
and I believe him on this—that it will not harm our
crew. It was, he said, "specifically designed for the
Emperor," and besides, they have no grudge against
us.*

Still, I have to confess that the thought of that unknown alien weapon sitting in our sickbay, force field around it or not, is an unsettling one.

Despite the deception of the Skedans, their cause is just. I have spoken with the leader of the Emperor's elite advisory council, Xanarit, and have arranged to have a private meeting with the Iora and Beytek. We have to work around the Tribute schedule, but Xanarit—to whom I have yet said nothing about the content of the discussion—has assured me that I will have a few moments alone with the Iora and Beytek. I will confront him and his council with his part in the demise of a peaceful, intelligent race of creatures. I understand that it's a risk. But then again, isn't every move we make out here in the Delta Quadrant a risk to some degree?

Seven of Nine will remain on board and continue her efforts to somehow understand and deactivate this weapon. The Doctor is providing security. Chakotay has the ship, and Tuvok, Neelix, and I will beam down for this Tribute.

I hope it's not too riotous a celebration.

Janeway grimaced at the sheer volume of all the excited, babbling voices. Any hope she might have had for a quiet, respectful observance had been dashed the moment they materialized on the planet.

"I love a good party," enthused Neelix, rubbing his hands together. "The Lhiaarians are such thorough bureaucrats that when they have a chance to relax and celebrate, they really enjoy it."

"I wish you'd thought to tell me that before," said

Janeway, grunting as a large reptilian body was jostled hard against her and then pulled away by the swell of the crowd.

Neelix looked hurt. "I sent you a full report yesterday, neatly entered in a padd, as per regulations."

"Sorry," said Janeway. "Guess I've been a little busy uncovering assassination plots and mind tricks."

"According to the information the Lhiaarian officials sent us," said Tuvok, "the Central Octagon, where the highlights of Tribute are being staged, is located half a kilometer in this direction. We are to arrive at the Southeast Gate, where Xanarit will greet us."

"Then let's go," said Janeway, unconsciously ducking her head as if to physically plow through the uncomfortable press of people. She wondered if anywhere in this vast Lhiaarian Empire there was a deserted planet—every place they'd stopped on this trek had been uncomfortably crowded.

Then she thought of Skeda, and remorse and anger flooded her. Murder wasn't the answer, though Tamaak might think so. But neither was sitting by and doing nothing. Janeway hoped desperately that she could make a difference. She realized that by confronting the Emperor in this matter, she might be sentencing her crew to the long way around Lhiaarian space, if not something worse. But she thought of young Priana, and the littlest Skedans, still sleeping in their mothers' pouches, and knew that there was, really, no choice at all.

It seemed to take forever to struggle down the crowded street, but finally they reached the meeting place. The Southeast Gate was huge and painted a bright blue color. Janeway put its age at several centuries, judging by the large amount of organic material.

"While the Lhiaarians do pride themselves on having the best and most advanced technology available to them," said Neelix, sounding like a travel guide, "the Central Octagon, where nearly all formal ceremonies are held, hasn't changed in over six hundred years. Routine repair work is of course performed and—"

"Neelix," said Janeway. She didn't have to say anything more.

They waited, as they had been told. Each second that ticked away was one more second in which Janeway could brood on what she was about to do, once she did indeed meet the Emperor face to face. When it was action that was required, Janeway was not one to postpone it, and this enforced period of waiting chafed at her.

"Captain Janeway," came a smooth, cultured voice. Janeway turned to see the familiar Lhiaarian visage—blue face-scales, black tongue, large eyes. "I am Xanarit. We spoke earlier. I must apologize for my tardiness. The sheer volume of those who have come to honor His Most Excellent Worthiness delayed me. I hope you have not been waiting long?"

"Not too long," Janeway replied. "When will we be able to have our private audience?"

Xanarit grimaced. "Not as soon as I had told you, I'm afraid. You are," and he consulted a small, handheld piece of equipment, "the fourth to petition Emperor Beytek. Ahead of you are the representatives from the Shamrik Moon and petitioners from Orlis Two, Four, and Eight. Considering there are thirty-seven, and the petitions will most likely continue throughout the night and well into tomorrow, you're actually in a good position."

"How fortunate for us," replied Janeway, keeping a forced smile on her face.

"I will leave one of my personal guards with you, and return for you when the Emperor is prepared to greet you. It is unfortunate that you have arrived during Tribute, when there are such demands on the Emperor's attention. According to custom, Beytek is not permitted to leave the Octagon until all the petitions are completed."

"I stipulated a private conversation," said Janeway.

"And private it shall be. I've arranged for you to meet in an area below the stage, away from the public eye. More I cannot do, unless you wish to wait a few days."

Janeway shook her head. "As long as I may speak freely and not be overheard by anyone save the Emperor and the Iora, a sequestered area below the stage will do." It had to.

Xanarit flicked his black tongue and dipped his head, then turned and was swallowed up by the crowd.

"It's going to be a long wait," said Janeway, sighing as she watched Xanarit go. "I hope everyone remembered to visit the head before we left."

* * *

Seven of Nine observed the results of yet another scan on the alien weapon. Nothing.

She glared at the radiant orb, as if somehow she could force it to yield its secrets by the very strength of her displeasure. But that was a foolish thought.

The twenty black birds watched her impassively. "Do you have any ideas?" she asked them sarcastically. One or two fluttered their wings, but they remained silent. They had come to her aid once before, helping her unlock the fragment of the nursery rhyme that had eventually led her to the discovery of this very weapon, but now the birds were silent and uncooperative.

She had searched her memories over and over again, but nothing she had learned about the Skedans had prepared her for this weapon. She suspected it was new, improvised technology, developed in the years since the Borg—since she—had assimilated the Skedans. The image of Rhiv, her eyes fastened on the hostile skies as she reached out in a futile gesture to save her children, appeared in Seven's mind. She blinked, hard, and deliberately banished the thought. Such emotions would not serve her now.

Seven went over what she did know. That the Skedans were able to generate mental, measurable energy in order to shape the thoughts of others, she knew. That this energy was now projected onto—and perhaps inside of—this orb, she suspected.

Any energy field had a frequency that generated it, and a frequency that could terminate it.

She just had to find it.

* * *

In Engineering, B'Elanna Torres moved fluidly, with a half-smile on her face. Whatever had been wrong with Tom was most decidedly not wrong anymore. He had been the perfect gentleman last night, taking her to the most romantic hologram program he'd ever designed for her—sunset on the beach of Talos IV. He'd ferried one of the native crafts along the shore, and they had swum in crystal clear waters. He'd even packed a picnic lunch with real food, using up half a week's worth of rations.

The perfect gentleman. Until the time had come when she hadn't *wanted* him to be the perfect gentleman and had let him know it in no uncertain terms.

Her mind on their wonderful evening, she moved through a routine maintenance chore.

Except she didn't press the proper buttons for routine maintenance on the warp core. Her fingers moved deftly over the special program she had created to adjust the Doctor's subroutine.

The Doctor was bored out of his skull. Or would have been, had he had an actual skeleton.

Seven of Nine was in sickbay—his sickbay—doing interesting experiments on the peculiar weapon, while he was stuck here staring at a closed door. There had been talk of stationing other security guards as well, but that had been dismissed. The Doctor never grew tired, could not be injured by attack, and was also the only person aboard *Voyager* who would not fall victim to a mental attack.

So here he was, by himself, his brilliant mind focused on watching the door to Cargo Bay One.

"What a waste," he said aloud, grumbling to no one.

Suddenly the door shimmered. Instantly alert, his hand went to the phaser at his hip. What were they doing to the door?

Then, in the space of a fraction of a second, he realized that there was nothing wrong with the cargo bay door. There was something wrong with him. He shimmered, and just before he winked out of existence, the door opened. Tamaak Vriis, followed by Imraak and Shemaak, burst through.

The Doctor opened his mouth to protest, reached to touch his commbadge, but he was too late.

He was gone.

CHAPTER
21

"WE HAVE NO DESIRE TO HARM YOU, BUT WE WILL USE this weapon if we must," came a voice.

Seven froze. Slowly, she turned around, knowing what she would see. Tamaak Vriis, the Skedan who had attacked her, Imraak, and Shemaak, the female who had come to her defense, stood in the doorway. Tamaak had a phaser pointed directly at her.

"Surely you mean, you have no desire to harm me further," she said, a hint of very human sarcasm in her voice.

Tamaak had the grace to look uncomfortable. Seven pressed her advantage. "Your species does not have experience with firing weapons of that kind," she replied coolly. "It is unlikely that you would hit me before I could disable you."

"It is on wide range," replied Tamaak. "And we have learned much since the Borg came and destroyed our world."

Seven's gaze flickered toward the sphere. "So it would seem."

"Step away from the weapon," Tamaak ordered. "I will use this if you force me to."

Seven did as she was instructed, but at the same moment her hand lifted toward her commbadge.

Tamaak watched Seven step backward, saw her hand lift, and knew what she was doing. He had no choice. He fired. She didn't utter a word, just crumpled to the floor.

"You should have killed her," muttered Imraak.

Tamaak's nerves were strained to the breaking point. He whirled on Imraak, aiming the weapon at him. "I should kill you!" he spat. "We have survived treachery and a Borg attack, but it took you to turn our people into monsters. You tried to force Seven to kill herself!"

"And it would be no great loss, to kill the thing who destroyed your family, would it?"

Tamaak's hand shook, but he kept the phaser pointed at Imraak. "It would be a great loss indeed," he said softly, "to fall so far, to stoop so low as to do what you have done."

Suddenly his rage was gone. Disgust filled him, and

he lowered the weapon. "We must deactivate the forcefield around it, then get it to the surface. Quickly. Help me."

Seven blinked. Her body tingled, but a quick assessment revealed that she was undamaged. Slowly, she sat up, and the memories came back. She glanced up—the weapon was gone, as she had suspected. In its place perched one of the twenty-one black birds. It blinked, then cawed loudly.

She ignored it and reached to touch her commbadge. It, too, was gone. The Skedans were thorough. She got to her feet, unsteadily, and strode toward the door.

She slammed into it. Rubbing her bumped nose, she realized exactly how thorough the Skedans had been. Even so, the most efficient course would have been for them to kill her.

My Tamaak would never condone that, came a thought, in a soft female voice that was not her own.

We're lucky then. Another thought that was not hers, from a determined young female who had watched the Borg mutilate her.

Fear spurted through Seven. She had thought these other lives gone, but they were still here. She smelled no choking stench of rot, and this time, the voices weren't distracting her with images of their own pain. They were helping her. It was as if she had unseen comrades, ready to share their advice and experience.

If so, they would be her only comrades for the near future. No one on *Voyager* would listen to her. They were unwitting pawns of the Skedans still on board. She could not rely on anyone save herself.

Seven assessed the situation. Tamaak and his companions had locked the door. She did not have the authority to override the computer system. There were no tools here in sickbay for repair work.

Then be creative—use your imagination! The old, raspy voice of an aging artist inside her mind.

Seven hurried to the tool kit and rummaged through it. She found an exoscalpel. "Crude, but efficient," she said aloud, and turned back toward the door. After all, a cutting tool was a cutting tool.

Several minutes later, Seven had raided the ammunition closet and was running full speed for the transporter room before the Skedans could trick someone into shutting that down, too. She had tried to communicate with Janeway and the away team on the surface, but the thorough Skedans had left nothing to chance. All communications with the away team had been severed, and the only way to warn them was to go to the surface herself.

The door to the transporter room hissed open. Fortunately, the room was empty. Seven hurriedly punched in the same coordinates as the away team, and stepped onto the platform. The transporter room shimmered about her for an instant, then she found herself in an open street.

Open, save for the thousands who crowded it. Seven fought back the urge to strike out and calmly pulled out a tricorder. Janeway, Tuvok, and Neelix were approximately a kilometer away. No one seemed to react to her presence, and indeed, in a place this crowded with representatives of so many places, Seven of Nine hardly stood out.

She adjusted the tricorder and nodded to herself. Tamaak, Imraak, and Shemaak were heading directly for the Central Octagon. Seven reached for her comm-badge automatically, to share the news of the danger with her captain, then lowered her hand as she remembered that Tamaak had taken her commbadge.

That settled it, then. Seven would follow the little band of terrorist Skedans alone. She did not wish to lose precious time.

It will be like stalking the skorrak bird, came an excited thought.

There are so many of them! sent Shemaak to her two companions.

Yes, Imraak replied. *So many of them and so very few of us now, thanks to them.*

Tamaak was weary of the incessant pounding of Imraak's hatred. *The average Lhiaarian knows nothing of what happened. They didn't even know there was a Borg attack, much less that Beytek covered up the incident. Cease blaming the race, Imraak. We know where the fault truly lies.*

He carried the precious Sphere and maneuvered his way through the crowd. No one even noticed them.

Years ago, when he and the rest of the Circle of Seven had devised the plan to exact revenge upon the Emperor, Tamaak had gone to sleep every night comforted with dreams of this hour. Now that the time had finally arrived, after much longer than any of them had expected, he felt no elation, only a grim sense of duty.

It would not bring his family back. But it would honor their memories. It would serve justice, and that would have to suffice.

The almost stunning blow of Shemaak's naked terror make Tamaak stumble. He whipped his head around, clutching the precious orb, and his own fear flooded him.

Not eight meters away, now revealed, now obscured by the tide of visitors for Tribute, stood the black, chitinous shape of a Ku. By the agitation of his body, Tamaak guessed the thing had seen them. The Ku were the only creatures Tamaak had ever encountered who naturally could not be affected by Skedan telepathy. Even the Borg needed their artificial implants to screen it out. But Ku brains were different, just as the Ku were different.

Not now. Not when they were so close—

Run. I will lead him astray.

Tamaak blinked, started at the thoughts Imraak sent. *If we are separated, you will die.* He tried and failed to cloak his imagination's depiction of just how Imraak would die.

Then my life will be ended, but our revenge will be won. Would that all decisions were this simple, this pure.

And then Imraak was gone, threading his way through the crowd, pausing just long enough to make certain the Emperor's assassin had been able to catch a clear glimpse. Shemaak and Tamaak watched for a moment, caught in horrified fascination. Then something broke in Tamaak and he pushed his companion forward.

Go! Do not let his sacrifice be in vain!

Imraak pushed his way through the crowds, heedless of the yelps and cries of annoyance and anger at his brusque manner. Now and then he craned his head back on his slender neck, just to make certain that the Ku had not lost sight of him. He needn't have worried. The giant insect sped along on six legs, entirely focused on the fleeing Skedan.

For a moment, Imraak wavered, although his feet did not slow. Had Tamaak been right? Had what he had tried to do to Seven of Nine been wrong?

Regardless, surely the Borg would be happy to see him now, fleeing yet not fleeing, trying to elude capture while all the time hoping for it.

I hope you learn of my death, somehow, he thought grimly. He had automatically directed his thoughts toward her, although he knew she would not be able to sense him from the distance of her vessel. Imraak was shocked and almost lost his footing when his thoughts brushed Seven's mind.

She was here. On the planet. No doubt in search of them. Any thoughts of remorse he might have had fled, drowned in a red tide of anger and panic. He was about to die for what he believed in, and she was here, with her accursed Borg implants, and she was trying to stop them.

He was about to concentrate his thoughts to send a final, murderous message—who cared now if Janeway discovered who had killed her pet Borg?—when agony rippled along his spine and he fell, hard. His nerves were jangled and he couldn't even lift his arm to break his fall.

In fact, he couldn't move at all. He was another victim of the Ku and their feared weapon, which paralyzed their prey until the time had come for their ritual of dismemberment—

Imraak stared wildly up at the insect as it bent over him. He could do nothing to harm his captor, but he could do something for himself. He had led the danger away from Tamaak and the precious weapon. Now, he could concentrate on mitigating his own pain.

He turned his thoughts inward, even as he felt himself being lifted as if he weighed nothing at all. He visualized his heart, beating rapidly with fear and exertion, and then he could actually see it.

Slow. Slow. Slow down, heart. Do not pump the warm blood that the Ku so despise. It is time for rest. You have beaten steadily every day of my life, but now, slow.

Slow.

Slow.

Stop.

CHAPTER
22

SEVEN OF NINE, HER BLUE-EYED GAZE FLICKERING FROM the tricorder to the streets ahead of her, strode as briskly as she could toward the Central Octagon. The Skedans were directly ahead. As she watched, one of them veered off in another direction. Frowning, Seven did a quick readjustment to the tricorder so that it picked up on the energy emanating from the Skedan's weapon.

The one who had left the group did not have the weapon. Seven dismissed him and continued following the remaining two.

Her eyes were on the instruments when she collided with something hard, that did not yield like the soft flesh of other beings she had hitherto encountered. Irritated, she glanced up.

And found herself staring into the multifaceted eyes of one of the Ku.

Species 13. Known among themselves as the Tuktak. Insectoid, able to adjust the density of their exoskeleton to comply with various environments. Hostile and intelligent.

Its antennae waved frantically and it emanated a bad scent. Seven tried not to wrinkle her nose at the peculiarly acrid smell. Though she had knowledge of them, thanks to the Collective, she had never personally encountered one before.

"A Warm," it said, its voice translated as harsh and mechanical. "A Borg warm. Better even. We will dismember and devour you, Warm, when our commander gives us the word."

"You are incorrect," said Seven calmly. She stepped forward, lifting the phaser. She knew exactly where to place it, between the compound eyes, and fired before the Tuktak even knew what had hit it. It dropped, its hard-shelled body clattering on the ancient paving stones of this street.

Gasps rose, but Seven ignored them. She began to run, a steady, non-tiring trot, shouldering her way roughly through anyone who dared attempt to stop her. She was going to lose the Skedans if she didn't hurry. And if she lost the Skedans, the Emperor was dead. Not that Seven particularly cared about the Emperor or the Skedan cause, but her captain did. Seven of Nine preferred to obey orders when possible, and this one she planned to carry out to the letter.

Her head suddenly ached. She felt the brush of an alien mind to hers and knew at once that the harsh thought came from the Skedan who had tried to induce her to suicide. Imraak. *I hope you learn of my death, somehow.*

Inside her, Rhiv mourned the death of yet one more of her people. Seven did not dare form a thought in reply, lest it reveal her presence to the others. She felt a peculiar sense of loss and knew that, although she felt it, the loss was not really hers. She moved on.

High overhead, almost invisible even to her eyes, flew twenty-two black birds. And inside her mind, speaking as if with one voice although they were many, Seven of Nine was kept company by every single being whom she had assimilated.

"The Emperor is finished with the present session. He'll be able to meet with you now," Xanarit told Janeway, nodding toward the huge stage on which the Emperor was seated and on which hundreds of petitioners had trod over the last few hours.

"Finally," muttered Janeway under her breath as she watched Emperor Beytek rise, wave to the crowd, and slip behind a fluttering black curtain. The sun on this planet was hot, and her hair and face were damp. She was probably also getting sunburned, but the Doctor would take care of that as soon as she returned to the ship. Neelix and Tuvok seemed to be experiencing no discomfort. Their captain silently envied them.

"Follow me, please." Xanarit marched forward, striding past the throngs of people who made no attempt to move past the small posts that designated the public area. Janeway, Neelix, and Tuvok followed. Xanarit's guards brought up the rear. As they walked, Janeway glanced about at the staggering array of monitors, cameras, and recording devices.

Publicity. Whatever its drawbacks, nothing small and vicious could survive long in the harsh glare of it, and Janeway intended to reveal the so-called Most Excellent Worthiness as little more than a spider in a web. Or a rat in a hole. Or a—her mind filled with metaphors and she smiled, slightly, to herself.

Xanarit led them past the steps that led up to the stage and through a doorway. Janeway blinked. Here beneath the stage, it was dark, and her eyes took a moment to grow accustomed to the dimness after the brightness of the sun. Once they were all inside, Xanarit closed the door. Abruptly, the noise of the crowd was utterly silenced.

"How secure is this room?" she asked, glancing about. There were no decorations, no colors here. The only furniture was a single chair. The walls were made of a gray substance unknown to her, and her voice sounded flat and hollow to her ears.

"Completely," Xanarit assured her. "Tribute has been held in the Central Octagon for centuries, and the Emperors have needed a place such as this where they may converse in privacy. Few places in the Empire are as secure as this antechamber, Captain. No sound, no weapon, nothing penetrates—and nothing leaves. I confess, I am curious as to the topic of your conversation with the Emperor, that you insist upon such privacy."

Janeway and Tuvok exchanged glances. She kept

her expression neutral, although her heart began to race.

"Commander, I've lost them," said Kim worriedly.

"What do you mean?" replied Chakotay.

"I mean, I've lost them. The transporter lock has been interrupted, the communications channel is being blocked—" He glanced up at Chakotay. "If there's trouble, they're on their own."

"Keep monitoring the situation, Ensign," Chakotay said at last. "Reestablish that lock at the first opportunity."

"Aye, sir."

Janeway made note of every inch of the room as she and her crew stood awaiting the arrival of the Emperor and his Iora. She hadn't wanted to come without a weapon, but it had been part of the terms of the meeting. She supposed she understood the precaution. You didn't get to talk to the head of Starfleet Command with a phaser on your hip, either, no matter who you were. But now things had taken an ominous turn. If the news she bore was not to the Emperor's liking, what was to stop him from executing the three *Voyager* crewmembers on the spot? No one would hear anything. It would be so easy.

She didn't think such a bureaucratic society would summarily execute them for what she was about to announce, but she couldn't be sure. That was a risk she and her crew were willing to take. What had been done to the Skedans was monstrous, and the Iora needed to know just what its adored Emperor had done to an innocent race. It was a task Janeway had to perform if she were ever to be able to sleep a whole night through again.

By twos and threes, the Iora entered, nodded at the Federation representatives, and stood stiffly behind the single chair. At last, the Emperor arrived. He strode into the room, head held high, robes fluttering, and seated himself in the chair.

"Captain Janeway," he said, his voice a purr. "You wished to see me?"

The moment had arrived. Janeway stuck her chin out and regarded Beytek. "I did. Thank you for granting us an audience. Xanarit has made us feel most welcome."

I can sense the quarry, came the happy thoughts of the youthful kitten. Seven nodded to herself. She could somehow sense them, too, though there was no logical means of explaining the knowledge.

A voice reached her ears and her head whipped up. "Thank you for granting us an audience. Xanarit has made us feel most welcome." The voice belonged to Captain Kathryn Janeway. It reverberated and echoed; in the back of her mind Seven analyzed the primitive communications system, thought of six ways to adjust it to improve performance, and dismissed it. She focused instead on the words, wondering why Janeway had changed her plan. The meeting was supposed to be private, and yet here was the captain, her face broadcast on the huge screens, her voice loud and clear.

"My crew and I have traveled far. We have seen

many worlds, met many people—even visited many empires. I must say that in my opinion, for as large and diverse as the Lhiaarian Empire is, it is extremely efficiently run."

Loud cheers and other noises of appreciation from the watching throngs. Seven quickened her pace. *For the maximum dramatic effect, Tamaak will strike at the moment when your captain reveals the depth of the Emperor's treachery.* The thought was from Druana, who knew such things.

Again, Seven nodded, as if the voice belonged to someone matching her stride for stride who could see and acknowledge the gesture. The thought crossed her mind that she was becoming used to these voices in her head. She didn't know if she should be comforted or disturbed.

They were directly ahead. Six meters. Something broke inside Seven and she shoved forcibly. "Let me through!" she cried, her voice rising. She was jostled and squeezed between bodies, and she knew that if she went down she might not get up again. She couldn't breathe and began to flail with her hands. Suddenly she was seized from behind, her slender arms pinned in a powerful grip.

Seven craned her neck to stare wildly at her captor. He was an enormous Lhiaarian guard, and his eyesacs were flushed a deep violet hue. Fury.

"Do you dare rush the Central Octagon when Tribute is under way?"

Faintly, Seven could still hear her captain talking. Janeway was still making pleasantries—readying the audience for the unpleasant truth to follow.

"Let me go," Seven demanded, reaching for calm. "I need to—"

"Very well." The guard released her so abruptly that she stumbled and barely caught herself. He turned like a robot and lumbered off in the opposite direction.

They're here! Keela's voice in her mind was loud and excited. Slowly, Seven of Nine turned.

Standing not a meter behind her was Tamaak Vriis and his companion. In Tamaak's slender arms, the unknown weapon, still glowing softly with its peculiar and inexplicable radiance, was cradled as tenderly as he might hold a pouchling.

"You diverted the guard," she said.

Tamaak nodded. "Yes. He would have hurt you. Badly, considering the temper he was in."

Seven narrowed her eyes even as she lifted the phaser and aimed it directly at Shemaak. With long fingers, Seven adjusted the setting to kill. She saw the comprehension dawn in both pairs of soft brown Skedan eyes.

"Give me the weapon," said Seven of Nine, fully in command, "or I will kill Shemaak where she stands."

CHAPTER
23

SLOWLY, TAMAAK SHOOK HIS HEAD. "NO," HE SAID, softly. "I will not surrender the weapon, and you will not kill Shemaak."

Puzzlement stayed Seven's hand. "I have killed before," she replied. "I will kill again. Why not Shemaak?"

"Because my mate is inside you," said Tamaak, "and she understands. *You* understand, too, Seven of Nine. All those inside you do."

"You are incorrect. I do not understand."

Tamaak Vriis half-closed his eyes in a Skedan smile. "Oh, yes you do. You know what this weapon is, and you, more than anyone else on this planet—in this empire—understand why we are here, doing what we are doing. Let us proceed."

"I have my orders."

"You have disobeyed them before, and you will again," Tamaak replied mildly, echoing her own words. "You can see through all the tricks I might attempt to play upon your mind. Therefore, I shall not attempt them. I only ask you to search your mind—your heart—and *know* that you know. Do then what you must. Neither of us will attempt to stop you. Destiny has come upon us, and all the fates have coalesced into this moment."

The phaser targeted on Shemaak did not waver. This was foolish. The weapon had been invented after the Borg had assimilated the Skedans, how could she possibly—

She shuddered. Rhiv, Tamaak's murdered mate, knew. Keela knew. So did Amari, and Druana, and To-Do-Ka, and Zarmuk, and Shrri. One by one, the selves that at this moment shared flesh with her realized what the ultimate consequence would be if Tamaak were permitted to use his weapon on the Emperor.

Seven felt something akin to panic. *What will it do? Tell me!*

But the selves in her mind were strangely silent.

All of a sudden, the twenty-three black birds flew past her. The wind from the beating of their wings would have stirred her hair had they been real. They hovered over the Skedans, cawing frantically. Seven lifted her eyes from her quarry to the birds, aching for their knowledge—for the knowledge that the Skedans insisted she possessed.

A murder of crows.

An unkindness of ravens.

The phaser fell from a suddenly nerveless hand to clatter on the cobblestones. Seven of Nine stared as comprehension burst upon her like an exploding star. For a moment, she felt as though her heart had ceased to beat, as if she were poised in a place where time had stopped.

"I . . . know . . . ," she whispered.

Sing a song of sixpence . . . .

Tamaak and Shemaak stayed silent, letting her wrestle with the sudden revelation. She took a deep, gasping breath, and stared at them. Finally, she was able to form words.

"Go," was all she said, in a voice as harsh as if she had been weeping all her life.

"It is clear to me that the Lhiaarian Empire boasts worlds of integrity and strength, and that the Lhiaarian people understand wisdom," said Janeway. The Iora looked pleased. Emperor Beytek, clad in garish scarlet-and-gold robes, was nodding his head. His eyesacs were orange—a sign of great pleasure.

Janeway wondered just what color they would turn at her next words.

No going back now.

"But sometimes the wisdom of a people does not manifest itself in their leaders."

Beytek's eyes narrowed. His black tongue flickered

out and he gestured to one of the guards standing erect against the wall. The guard pressed a button and a hidden door slid open. Standing in the doorway, mandibles clicking and antennae waving, were three Ku.

Janeway's mouth suddenly went dry and the words died in her throat. She stared at the Ku, then at Beytek. He'd known. He'd known all along.

"Is this how you handle those who would speak the truth?" she managed, anger welling up to chase away the fear.

"It is how I handle liars," said Beytek mildly. "I am only sorry you didn't bring Tamaak Vriis down with you. But then again, I would so hate depriving my loyal allies the Ku of their pleasure. Your vessel will not stand, Captain. The Ku will board it, and claim you and the Skedans."

"You were expected, Captain Janeway," said Xanarit. "We knew that you carried the Skedans, that you knew the truth. Or did you? What did they tell you?"

"They told me that the Borg attacked their planet," said Janeway, anger fueling her words. She warmed to her task, spitting the words out, needing to say them even if they fell on deaf ears, needing to be the voice that spoke truth until it was silenced by her own death. Out of the corner of her eye, Janeway saw Tuvok and Neelix straighten and steel themselves for a fight—a fight that would probably end in their deaths. She was terribly proud of them.

"That Beytek promised to send reinforcements and didn't, that he let millions of innocent people die rather than attack the Borg and reveal the power of the Empire. The Skedans were assimilated and murdered, and the few who were left were branded infected. Even after his betrayal of his own people, good and loyal citizens of the Empire, Beytek would not lift a single claw to help them."

Beytek shrugged. "Unfortunate. But what else was I to do, Captain? Some must die so that others might live. I couldn't have the Borg turning their attention to Lhiaari. And any Skedans who survived would have told what had happened. That would be very bad publicity for me and my Empire, wouldn't it?"

"Dreadful publicity," said Xanarit. "Public opinion would topple the Emperor from his seat."

"Indeed it would," agreed Beytek.

"Indeed it will," replied Xanarit. "Janeway! Go!"

In a whirlwind of motion, the guards who had had their weapons trained on Janeway, Tuvok, and Neelix suddenly thrust weapons into their hands. A panel slid open behind their backs. Janeway snapped out of her instant of shock and began firing at the approaching Ku. The weapons didn't seem to cause injury, but the smash of energy into their chitinous bodies did slow them, allowing Janeway and her crew precious time to clamber up the dark stairs.

The Ku were right behind them. She could hear their angry chittering, hear Tuvok and Neelix firing as they went. She slammed her head against a panel at the top of the steps and, clutching the alien weapon on one hand, fumbled to open the door with the other.

Light assaulted her eyes. She blinked and climbed out. The roaring nearly deafened her and she realized that they had emerged directly onto the central stage area. She stared, shocked, at the image of her own face on the huge viewscreen. The Ku followed them, but the guards followed the Ku. There was a brief skirmish, then the Ku were trapped on all sides by Imperial guards. Beytek was the next to emerge from below the stage, his face angry and frightened. Xanarit and the Iora, weapons drawn and pointed at their Emperor, followed.

At that moment, the sun went out.

Seven had dropped to the ground and was curled up in a tight ball. She leaned against the cool comfort of an ancient stone wall, out of the way, for the moment, of trampling feet. She shuddered, and clutched her knees to her chest. Her eyes were squeezed shut, but behind the closed lids she saw the scene play itself out. She had the company of thousands in her mind.

A pocket full of rye . . .

Screams of terror exploded from the crowd in the hot darkness. As suddenly as it had descended, the darkness lifted, but natural sunlight did not return. The illumination came from a single glowing orb—a sphere that Janeway recognized. Hovering in the air was Tamaak Vriis, the dreadful weapon clutched in his arms.

As the wonderful scent of brewing coffee hit her nostrils, Janeway realized what was going on. The sun hadn't really gone out, nor was Tamaak suddenly able to fly. This was Skedan mind manipulation, and Janeway wondered if everyone assembled saw the same vision that she did or if the experience was different for each individual. The event was being recorded, and the Skedans could not alter that. When this was over, if she survived, she would be able to see what had actually transpired.

"Xanarit!" she yelled. "The Skedan—it's a trick! He's planning to kill the Emperor!"

Xanarit looked at her, startlingly calm given the hysteria surrounding him, and merely nodded.

"What Captain Janeway has said about the destruction of Skeda is the truth!" Tamaak's voice boomed forth like the voice of God on Judgment Day— another illusion, but a frighteningly compelling one. "You have even seen the oh-so-noble Emperor Beytek the Seventh confess to it! He has shamed his ancestors and the people he dares to call subjects. He promised to send ships to defend us—none came. And then we were even cut off from any assistance from other quarters. Left to die, and be forgotten, save as foul plague spreaders to be shunned for as long as we lived.

"But you cannot elude justice, Beytek. It will find you. It will seek you out. I am one of the last of my people and we have long dreamed of this day. Fear, Beytek. Your hour has come at last. Behold the orb of judgment!"

Seven saw it all. Saw the illusion of the flying Tamaak, the naked terror and cowardice upon the Emperor's features, the calm visage of Xanarit, the anger and fear for another's safety that shone in Janeway's face. Inside her mind, thousands of voices cried out for justice, and twenty-three birds shrieked wildly.

Four and twenty blackbirds baked in a pie . . .

With a cry, Tamaak lifted the glowing orb above his head, then sent it hurtling downward. Janeway felt a useless scream of warning tear from her throat. She ran forward, though she didn't know what she hoped to accomplish. It was pure instinct, an attempt to try to stop the inevitable.

Surely it was a bomb of some sort. It would be the last thing she saw before death finally claimed her and she would truly be exploring that most final of frontiers. She'd looked death in the face so often it was almost difficult to believe it had finally come.

Part of her was enraged that Tamaak would so slay thousands of innocents. She had thought more of him than that. But here was the proof, falling slowly toward the stage to crash and explode at the Emperor's feet.

It crashed. It did not explode.

The orb shattered like glass. Shards flew everywhere and a radiant mist rose upward like smoke—smoke with a life of its own. It twined and writhed, and as she watched it headed straight for Beytek. It forced itself into his nose, eyes, and mouth, almost raping him. He bent backwards, taut with agony, but was utterly silent.

And then he was not.

His mouth yawned open almost impossibly wide, and the most dreadful sounds Janeway had ever heard, ever dreamed, issued forth. They pierced her very soul. Janeway opened her mouth in a soundless cry of pain and fell hard to her knees, clutching her ears as the incarnation of agony continued to assault her.

They were screams, but more than that: they were the shrieks not just of voices, but of the mind and soul. She knew at once without knowing how she knew just what she was listening to: the last sounds and thoughts and feelings of billions of Skedans as they helplessly watched the end of their world.

She curled up on the stage, unable to help herself, and scalding tears of empathy were ripped from her eyes. Janeway couldn't breathe, could only sob helplessly, as caught up in the power of Tamaak's weapon as a fly in a spider's web.

Around her, others reacted in a similar fashion. She had never thought to hear the sound of Tuvok weeping.

When the pie was opened, the birds began to sing . . . wasn't that a tasty dish to set before the king?

Alone of all the thousands witnessing the havoc wrought by Tamaak's weapon, Seven wept with fierce joy. *This* was what the nursery rhyme meant. *This* was what the appearance of four and twenty blackbirds had signified. All along, somehow, she had been aware of the presence of the weapon, and of what it would do.

The pie had been opened and the blackbirds were singing indeed, singing with the voices of the most innocent, who had suffered untold agonies. And it was a tasty dish indeed for the Emperor, who had deliberately and single-handedly caused it all. Everyone present, even those watching on a vidscreen, could hear the cries, mental and physical, of the dying.

But Beytek, alone of all of them, *was feeling everything*.

Tears from her single true eye coursed down her face. She lifted her head and saw the twenty-four blackbirds wheeling in a tight circle. Then, one by one in a succession so rapid it took only seconds, Seven felt the people whose memories she had shared depart.

Now she sobbed in pain, in the abrupt sensation of solitude after days of the company of thousands. She was alone, again. The birds flew faster and faster, until they blurred in her tearful vision and coalesced into another shape—the shape of one little girl.

Annika Hansen laughed and twirled delightedly, the skirt of her white dress flying about her like wings. Her blond curls bobbed, and when she came to a stop, she looked right at Seven of Nine. She smiled, revealing tiny, perfect teeth, placed her hands to her lips, and blew Seven of Nine a kiss.

Then she was gone.

CHAPTER
24

THE SILENCE PRESSED ON JANEWAY'S EARS LIKE SOME-
thing physical. She felt as though her body weighed a
thousand kilos as she struggled to lift her head and
brush the hair out of her eyes.

"Beytek," she rasped. Beside her, Tuvok and Neelix
struggled to their feet, seemingly as drained as she.

Beytek stood where she had last seen him. He might
have been carved from stone, so still was he. His eyes
were wide, his mouth still yawning open although now
he was frighteningly silent. A thin, silver trail of
spittle dripped from his lips. His eyesacs were cold
gray.

"Is he dead?" Janeway asked.

Tamaak Vriis, accompanied by Shemaak, stepped into her vision. "No," he replied in a voice that quivered with exhaustion. "But his mind is gone. He may recover in a few years, but for now, he can harm no one further. You heard the deaths of our people, Captain. He experienced it."

An old saying flashed into Janeway's mind: *Let the punishment fit the crime.* She had wronged Tamaak by believing that he would drag innocents into his revenge. The weapon, which now looked like so much broken glass, had been targeted for one person, that Beytek might experience the same fate that he put billions through.

She still would not have let Tamaak use the weapon, had she known. Justice needed to be accomplished through legal means, not eye-for-an-eye revenge.

But she couldn't argue with the deep satisfaction she felt in her belly.

Tamaak lifted his hands in a universal gesture of surrender. He turned to Xanarit. "I will take whatever punishment you decree. All of my people will. We have lived only to see this hour, and now, all is done."

Xanarit looked dreadful. His eyesacs were bright green as he shook his head.

"No. We have wronged your people, Tamaak Vriis. I had hoped to facilitate your meeting with him here in public. I didn't know about . . . ." His voice trailed off as he stared at the living shell of his Emperor.

"It was you," breathed Janeway, comprehension dawning as she stared at Xanarit. "You saved us from the Ku, got us the audience with Emperor Beytek. You told us—you said we had friends on Lhiaari."

Xanarit nodded. "Yes, Captain Janeway. I knew who you were and who you were bringing. I apologize for tricking you, but it was the only way I could contrive on such short notice to see justice done. Nothing you said in the antechamber was private. I had set it up so that everything that transpired would be heard and seen by everyone in the Empire. I knew you would confront Beytek with what you had learned, and that he would confess to it. I had hoped to promote understanding, reveal the secret, force Beytek to acknowledge the crime he committed and . . . what is done, is done. The Emperor is no longer fit to lead, and as the head of the Iora, I must shoulder his responsibilities."

He turned around, to face the crowd gone strangely silent. The recording devices were still on. Xanarit now had the complete attention of billions.

"Emperor Beytek is still alive," he said, his voice clear and strong. He stood erect—the perfect image of a just leader. "What we all underwent was a powerful telepathic experience, sent to our minds by Tamaak Vriis, a Skedan. We all heard what it was like to witness the destruction of millions. Emperor Beytek, whose actions caused such terror and death, actually experienced what we merely heard. His mind could not stand it.

"Tamaak and his people have been horribly wronged. While I do not agree with the method they have chosen to seek their justice, I will, as my first deed as acting Emperor, petition the Iora and the people to pardon him."

He held out his arms to the crowd beseechingly. Noise now began to ripple through the crowd. Not the angry growl of a discontented mob, but the low murmur of agreement. Janeway saw Xanarit's shoulders relax ever so slightly. He was in line with what his people wanted, as a good leader must be.

"There are a few Skedans who survived Beytek's treachery. I believe I speak for all Lhiaarians when I say we welcome them to our homeworld with eyesacs of blue. If Lhiaari has anything to do with it, Tamaak, your people will survive. Beytek's actions, taken without consulting the Iora, shamed the whole Empire. And that Empire will do all it can to make restitution. Let this day be a day of healing."

He reached out his clawed hands to Tamaak. Stunned, for a moment the Skedan could only stare. Then his splendid eyes closed in a smile and he reached out his own paws to clasp those of Xanarit.

No more fear, no more death, no more burning revenge. Beytek stirred, blinking foolishly, not comprehending what was transpiring.

Janeway thought that a pity.

The Doctor snapped his tricorder shut with an air of finality. "Congratulations, Seven. I detect no further hyperstimulation of the limbic system. You are fit as a fiddle."

She stared at him, narrowing her eyes. "A fiddle is another word for a violin—an instrument. How can an inanimate object be considered to be in prime physical condition when—"

"Looks like you're right, Doctor," Janeway interrupted with a smile. "That's our Seven."

"The birds are gone, then?" asked Chakotay.

Seven nodded. "Yes."

"Seven," began Janeway, choosing her words carefully, "do you—do you still have the memories of—"

"Those I assimilated?" The thought stirred nothing within Seven but cool analysis. "No. I remember having them, but—It is like eating Neelix's food. You remember consuming the nutrients, but after a while the actual physical substance does not linger in the body."

"I spoke briefly with Tamaak Vriis. Without the Skedans' direct manipulation of Seven's memory centers, the memories will subside back into her subconscious," said the Doctor. "Perhaps one day, Seven will be able to access them on her own."

"Why should I wish to do that?"

Janeway stepped forward and put a gentle hand on Seven's shoulder. "To learn from them, Seven. Those people—Keela, Druana, the others—they are all a part of you. They have things to teach you."

Seven's gaze flickered from Janeway's hand on her shoulder to her captain's eyes. "I know their technological and cultural knowledge. I need to learn nothing more."

Janeway's hand fell away. She glanced quickly at Chakotay, then back at Seven. "Perhaps you're right, Seven. Now that you're back to—well, normal, for you—perhaps you can tell me what you were doing down on the surface without your commbadge."

Crisply and succinctly, Seven related what had transpired both on the ship and on the surface. She edited nothing, apologized for nothing, wrestled for words that were accurate and not full of the sort of emotional charge to which both Janeway and Chakotay seemed to respond so powerfully. They didn't interrupt her, merely watched her face, her body language. For what, Seven didn't know.

"You let Tamaak Vriis proceed?" asked Chakotay.

"That is what I said," replied Seven.

"Clearly, Tamaak was still somehow managing to manipulate her mind," Janeway said. "The detonation of the—mind bomb, I suppose you could call it—must have released the last traces of Skedan influence from Seven's mind."

"Do not speak of me as if I were not present," said Seven, annoyance creeping into her voice. "And do not make such unfounded assumptions."

"But the birds," said Janeway. "They didn't stop manifesting until the bomb exploded."

"The birds had nothing to do with Tamaak's presence in my mind," said Seven. "I called them, somehow. The Doctor says they were manifestations of my subconscious."

"On her own, without mental interference, Seven would have immediately sensed the presence of the Skedans' bomb," interjected the Doctor. "She needed to be distracted, so Tamaak and friends pulled the memories of those Seven had assimilated to occupy her thoughts. The raven has appeared before, sort of as a herald of knowledge that Seven was unaware she possessed. It performed that function again, fighting to be acknowledged by Seven's conscious mind, except this time it brought along twenty-three pals."

"There were twenty-four birds to evoke the nursery rhyme in my mind," continued Seven. "As the last few lines read, when the pie was opened—when the bomb was detonated—the birds began to sing."

"The Skedan voices of the dead issued forth," said Tuvok, nodding. "Quite logical."

"You knew what you were doing?" asked Janeway. Seven nodded.

"You disobeyed a direct order! We didn't know what that weapon was. It could have killed thousands of—"

"I knew what it was," said Seven coldly. "Captain, there have been times when you have found me in Master Leonardo's studio. We have had—discussions. You have often told me that one day I would understand an elusive concept called compassion. Are you sorry I learned your lessons so well?"

Janeway was speechless. Then, finally, she found her voice. "For the record," she said in an icy voice, "I will continue to believe that you were under the influence of alien mental commands until the moment that mind-bomb was detonated. You were not yourself. Is that understood?"

Something flared in Seven's chest, burned brightly, then subsided. "Completely, Captain."

"Good. I'm giving you the rest of your shift off. Report to your regular duties at 0600 tomorrow."

Without another word, Janeway turned and strode

out. Chakotay gave Seven a last, reassuring smile, and followed.

"What do I do, Chakotay?" said Janeway softly as they entered the turbolift and headed for the bridge. "What do I say to her? How can I condone what she did—but on the other hand, how can I condemn it?"

"I realize those are probably rhetorical questions, so I'll let you puzzle them out," her first officer and friend replied, smiling a little.

"She disobeyed orders—but out of compassion, if she's to be believed," Janeway continued, speaking more to herself. "Was it true? Has this incident given Seven a conscience?"

"That's the big question. We'll just have to wait and see." Chakotay seemed to want to say more, but fell silent.

"Out with it," chided Janeway teasingly, already feeling better simply by being in his reassuring, calm presence.

"I think the Doctor may be wrong about the black bird."

"Really?"

He nodded. "If there has ever been anyone who needed assistance—who needed a friend, a guide, if you will—surely then it was the child Annika Hansen. I think she's found one. The black bird may be Seven's animal spirit, come to her without her even knowing or seeking it."

Janeway felt gooseflesh erupt all over her body. Even her hair prickled. She forced her voice to be calm, light, even, as she spoke.

"I wonder what Edgar Allan Poe would say about this."

It was lunchtime in the mess hall, and the air was filled with the buzz of conversation. Seven was surrounded by her fellow crewmen, but she felt utterly alone.

They were gone. The twenty-four black birds were not perched atop crewmen's heads and shoulders and filling the room to capacity with their inky, mysterious presences. The voices of the thousands who had shared her mind and body over the past few days were silent. She didn't dare try to call them to her again, not so soon, but she ached inside with a fierce emptiness she had not known since she had first been forcibly separated from the Collective.

One mind in one body. The individual. It was so terribly isolating.

Janeway had uttered the confusing phrase "not yourself." What did that even mean? What was it *to* be oneself? She was reminded of Paris's vast vocabulary of slang and resolved to ask him about it.

Who was she, now? Before? Ever?

Was she Annika Hansen? Seven of Nine, Tertiary Adjunct of Unimatrix Zero-One? Just plain Seven? And who *was* just plain Seven?

A soft harumph distracted her. She glanced up to see Neelix standing playfully at attention. "It's my understanding that my friend Seven is finally back with us. It'd be my pleasure to get her whatever her heart—or her stomach—desires."

My friend Seven. The whole concept of "friend"

was a mammoth one. One best left, perhaps, for another time.

Seven of Nine was silent for a moment. Then, surprising herself, she knew what she wanted. "I think," she said, slowly and deliberately, "I would like a piece of chocolate cake."

"Coming right up!" Grinning broadly, Neelix scurried away to fetch her the pastry.

My friend Seven. Seven of Nine. I. Me.

Just plain Seven.

For now, it would have to do.

ABOUT THE AUTHOR

Christie Golden is the author of ten novels and over a dozen short stories. Among her credits are two other *Voyager* novels, *The Murdered Sun* and *Marooned,* as well as two original novels, *Instrument of Fate* and *King's Man & Thief* from Ace Books. On the strength of *The Murdered Sun,* Golden now has an open invitation to pitch for *Voyager,* the show. She also wrote the novelization and first original tie-in, *On the Run,* for the Steven Spielberg–produced animated television show *Invasion America.*

Golden lives in Colorado with her husband and two cats. Readers are encouraged to visit her web site at: www.sff.net/people/Christie.Golden.

Look for STAR TREK Fiction from Pocket Books

Star Trek: The Next Generation®

Star Trek: Deep Space Nine®

Star Trek®: Voyager™

Flashback • Diane Carey
Mosaic • Jeri Taylor
The Black Shore • Greg Cox

#1 *Caretaker* • L. A. Graf
#2 *The Escape* • Dean W. Smith & Kristine K. Rusch
#3 *Ragnarok* • Nathan Archer
#4 *Violations* • Susan Wright
#5 *Incident at Arbuk* • John Greggory Betancourt
#6 *The Murdered Sun* • Christie Golden
#7 *Ghost of a Chance* • Mark A. Garland & Charles G. McGraw
#8 *Cybersong* • S. N. Lewitt
#9 *Invasion #4: The Final Fury* • Dafydd ab Hugh
#10 *Bless the Beasts* • Karen Haber
#11 *The Garden* • Melissa Scott
#12 *Chrysalis* • David Niall Wilson
#13 *The Black Shore* • Greg Cox
#14 *Marooned* • Christie Golden
#15 *Echoes* • Dean W. Smith & Kristine K. Rusch
#16 *Seven of Nine* • Christie Golden

Star Trek®: New Frontier

#1 *House of Cards* • Peter David
#2 *Into the Void* • Peter David
#3 *The Two-Front War* • Peter David
#4 *End Game* • Peter David
#5 *Martyr* • Peter David
#6 *Fire on High* • Peter David

Star Trek®: Day of Honor

Book One: *Ancient Blood* • Diane Carey
Book Two: *Armageddon Sky* • L. A. Graf
Book Three: *Her Klingon Soul* • Michael Jan Friedman
Book Four: *Treaty's Law* • Dean W. Smith & Kristine K. Rusch

Star Trek®: The Captain's Table

Star Trek®: The Dominion War

1252.01

STAR TREK
DEEP SPACE NINE

24" X 36" CUT AWAY POSTER.
7 COLORS WITH 2 METALLIC INKS & A GLOSS AND MATTE VARNISH. PRINTED ON ACID FREE ARCHIVAL QUALITY
65# COVER WEIGHT STOCK INCLUDES OVER 90 TECHNICAL CALLOUTS. AND HISTORY OF THE SPACE STATION.
U.S.S DEFIANT EXTERIOR. HEAD SHOTS OF MAIN CHARACTERS. INCREDIBLE GRAPHIC OF WORMHOLE.

STAR TREK™
U.S.S. ENTERPRISE™ NCC-1701

24" X 36" CUT AWAY POSTER.
6 COLORS WITH A SPECIAL METALLIC INK & A GLOSS AND MATTE VARNISH. PRINTED ON ACID FREE ARCHIVAL
QUALITY 100# TEXT WEIGHT STOCK INCLUDES OVER 100 TECHNICAL CALLOUTS.
HISTORY OF THE ENTERPRISE CAPTAINS & THE HISTORY OF THE ENTERPRISE SHIPS.

ALSO AVAILABLE:

LIMITED EDITION SIGNED AND NUMBERED BY ARTISTS.
LITHOGRAPHIC PRINTS ON 80# COVER STOCK (DS9 ON 100 # STOCK) WITH OFFICIAL LICENSED CERTIFICATE OF
AUTHENTICITY. QT. AVAILABLE 2,500

STAR TREK

AVAILABLE
NOV 1996
U.S.S. ENTERPRISE™ 1701-E
CUTAWAY $19.95
LTD. ED SIGNED & # PRINTS QT 2,500
$40.00

SCIPUBTECH

Deep Space Nine Poster
Poster Qt.___ @ $19.95 each _____
Limited Edition Poster
Poster Qt.___ @ $40.00 each _____

U.S.S. Enterprise NCC-1701-E Poster
Poster Qt.___ @ $19.95 each _____
Limited Edition Poster
Poster Qt.___ @ $40.00 each _____

U.S.S. Enterprise NCC-1701 Poster
Poster Qt.___ @ $14.95 each _____
Limited Edition Poster
Poster Qt.___ @ $30.00 each _____
$4 Shipping U.S. Each _____
$10 Shipping Foreign Each _____
Michigan Residents Add 6% Tax _____
TOTAL _____

METHOD OF PAYMENT (U.S. FUNDS ONLY)
❏ Check ❏ Money Order ❏ MasterCard ❏ Visa
Account #

_ _ _ _ - _ _ _ _ - _ _ _ _ - _ _ _ _

Card Expiration Date ___ /___ (Mo./Yr.)

Your Day Time Phone (___) - _____

Your Signature

SHIP TO ADDRESS:

NAME:_____

ADDRESS:_____

CITY:_____STATE:_____

POSTAL CODE:_____COUNTRY:_____

Mail, Phone, or Fax Orders to:
SciPubTech • 15318 Mack Avenue • Grosse Pointe Park • Michigan 48230
Phone 313.884.6882 Fax 313.885.7426 Web Site http://www.scipubtech.com

ST5196